By Fielding Dawson

Stories & Dreams:

Krazy Kat/The Unveiling (1969)
The Dream/Thunder Road (1972)
The Sun Rises Into the Sky (1974)
The Man Who Changed Overnight (1976)
Krazy Kat & 76 More, Collected Stories 1950–1976
 (1982)
Tiger Lilies: an American childhood (1984)
Virginia Dare, Stories 1976–1981 (1985)
Will She Understand? New Short Stories (1988)
The Orange in the Orange: A Novella and Two
 Stories (1995)

Novels:

Open Road (1970)
The Mandalay Dream (1971)
A *Great* Day for a Ballgame (1973)
Penny Lane (1977)
Two Penny Lane (1977)
Three Penny Lane (1981)

Memoirs:

An Emotional Memoir of Franz Kline (1967)
The Black Mountain Book (1970)
The Black Mountain Book, *A New Edition* (1991)

Poetry:

Delayed, Not Postponed (1978)

FIELDING DAWSON

THE ORANGE IN THE ORANGE

A NOVELLA & TWO STORIES

BLACK SPARROW PRESS
SANTA ROSA • 1995

ACKNOWLEDGMENTS

Photos by Fielding Dawson and Susan Maldovan.

Black Sparrow Press books are printed on acid-free paper.

LIBRARY OF CONGRESS CATALOGING-IN-PUBLICATION DATA

Dawson, Fielding, 1930–
    The orange in the orange : a novella and two stories / Fielding
Dawson.
        p.   cm.
    Contents: Under the trees on the hill — The orange in the orange
— Hands like Titian's Venus.
    ISBN 0-87685-963-5 (cloth trade) : $25.00. — ISBN
0-87685-962-7 (pbk.) : $13.50. — ISBN 0-87685-964-3 (signed
cloth) : $35.00
    1. Creative writing—Study and teaching—Fiction.
2. Prisoners as authors—Fiction.   3. Prisons—Fiction.   I. Title.
PS3554.A948O7   1995
813'.54—dc20   94-45314
                                                                CIP

It is a thing to have
A lion, an ox in his breast,
To feel it breathing there.

Poetry Is a Destructive Force
Wallace Stevens

CONTENTS

Under the Trees on the Hill

In the first week of the last month of the semester, a new young convict came into the classroom, took a seat and watched the teacher with sharp eyes. Soon he was involved in discussions — even wrote essays, original stuff, quick — zipped them off, so smart. Sharp, and charming, good looking yet warm, yet an edge of violence. Soon embroiled in one of those classroom stews where everybody speaks, yells, shouts, demands, implores and teacher helpless, let it go, to witness and enjoy it: that afternoon loud and fervent on their neighborhoods and what who wanted to be most or — something, life's ambition not often clear in these prison debates, but of a sudden the new fellow's voice rose, and took command. So compelling teacher lost sense of the classroom . . . they were on a street corner, and he listened to this vivid tale of woe, told with verve, wit and sparkle, in the most intense angry amusement:

". . . you know that street that goes up a hill overlooking the river, near the academy?"

"Oh yes," teacher smiled, glancing at the other guys, seated in their desks, listening.

"That's where I saw her car!" cried the youth. "You know, those trees along the sidewalk?"

Guys nodded.

"Yes." Teacher.

11

"Well, that's where I saw her car, parked. I knew her car."

"Okay."

Knowing something was coming, teacher looked at the guys, and grinned. They too. Grinned.

"In front of his house," he said, bending a little, being slender, and small, as if to stretch himself longer, tense in anger and laughter, excited: eyes wide, pupils floating. Arms outstretched, fingers spread—"His house! The guy she was in love with! *He* was a cop! *I* wasn't, but she," he laughed, wild, "she *wanted* to be a cop, *she wanted me to be a cop,* and—"

"Was parked in front of his house," teacher said, lips in a smile. Eyes not.

"*Yeah*! Because he was a cop! I saw her car. I know her car, and it was there, under the trees on the hill in front of the house where the *cop* lived!"

And a couple of weeks later, shook hands in that room, and said goodbye . . . the end of the last class before graduation ceremonies . . . sad, to say farewell. Teacher gave him his address saying keep in touch, sure! Sure! Knowing he never would and he was right, for the youth did not, but why, in truth, should he? Aside from the fact he had come into teacher's poetry class, and teacher had paid attention to him, what did that say, or do? Teacher was not the essential point. How the young man was responding to the car under the trees on the hill. That was the image, the poetic image, and the story without a plot told by an unedu-cated but talented, very intelligent, very angry and perhaps too insecure youth, in a passing two or three classes, in the School Block, in a House of Detention for Men, in a big city somewhere, anywhere in America, a country where saying goodbye was tough, it hurt, but it was said more often than saying hello, and getting more and more the thing to do, the way things were going.

Teacher stood there, facing the empty chairs, in the empty classroom, looking out the dirty windows at the dry, gray, weedy ground between cell blocks, under a low even dirtier sky. He had learned to let these guys go. He had to let them go where they would, wherever it was, because he was not the essential.

True.

But teacher was a resolute and caring man, and to let them go infuriated him — he knew he was not the essential, home and family were — but letting them go as if to the winds angered him because he remembered them all, thus they were memorable, and they *were* in the notes he kept, so they were in his way *of him*. This anger was in his eyes, in the set, determined expression of his lips, and across his face which caused certain prison guards to look twice at him, with murder in their longing eyes, because he hated them, and held them in contempt. Thus he wore his face in mask, so they looked at him and saw no one. A deception teaching in prisons had taught him, and he had learned, fast.

The Orange in the Orange

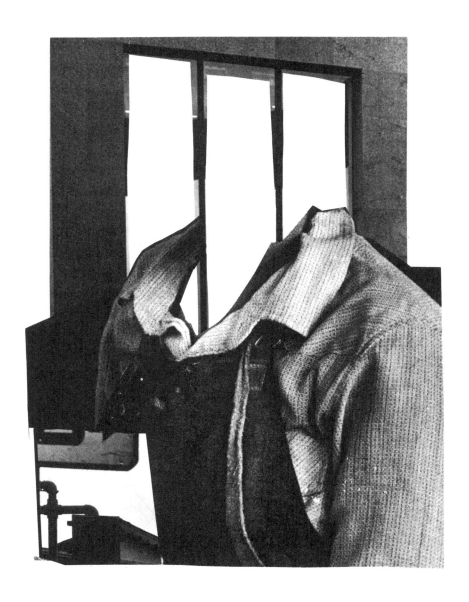

In memory of the sons, of the young men alive, and dead and alive — or dying, but alive with a chance to stay *alive: all of them, in particular Jim Dawson, my son. Died: AIDS, January, 1986. Gifted writer, artist, musician . . . I was not much of a father, and want this book, and those to follow, to be in his memory, his, with the living sons I work with, behind high walls, everywhere.*

"Listen, in the distance there's a town. A town with men, free men, and women, babies, and movie shows, and hot dog stands, and autos. But we can't see the town. All we can see is land, land, and more land, and a gray horizon dragging across our eyes.

"It's raining. Not cats and dogs—but a drizzle, just a steady drizzle. It's raining to you, maybe, and it's raining to the deacons and the jaunty young men in new straw hats and to the slim, pretty women in fresh, bright dresses. It's raining to *Mister* Charley, and his wife, and his son, and his daughters. It's raining to farmer Jones and blacksmith Joe. But it ain't raining to us convicts in the fields. Setting out sweet potato vines in the rain. That's no song. Hell, that ain't nothing. But convicts, setting out potatoes in the rain. Red mud sticking to our heavy shoes and the bottoms of our ragged overalls until our feet are just part of an acre of ground.

"Listen, there's a little chill in the rain, left over from March. When our overalls and jumpers get wet clear through we can feel the chill in the rain on our ribs. On our separate ribs. You can see 'em, too, not the overalls, but our ribs, our separate ribs when the overalls get wet in the rain. And stick."

In the Rain
Chester Himes

MONDAY IN LOVE

The sky was big and blue, and made for the rich, just as the promo said: a great place to Cross Over. That tall sign in the park, the smaller one in front of the main office, and on the letterheads, business cards, in the Yellow Pages — quarter page ad each issue of *Modern Maturity Magazine*.

The logo a silver bridge, going from the top of a green hill into a white cloud. Letters, along the bottom, in stylish script: CROSSOVER ACRES. Birds singing, brook rippling, flowers under a happy sun.

The location on the edge of the city nearest the mountains: a new development, its own hospital, post office, shopping center, library . . . handsome condo-world for wealthy seniors who returned from Florida and Arizona, to die at home.

Right across the street, a new park faced the main office and entrance. On its eastern edge was a row of very pretty, very clean and very expensive one and two-storey, chrome and blue-glassed, air-modulated, entrances to plush, quiet, specialty shops for seniors and pets. So that on a nice day the park was a pleasant sight with nurses and middle-aged children wheeling parents, or keeping step with walkers, on smooth, black asphalt paths between trees, bushes, bright flower beds, with soft, comfy, plastic benches beside well-tended small hills, streams, and pools with frogs and fish, in sound and scent, recalling the happy days of childhood past, in a cleaner, simpler, more easy-going world, than the other one that surrounded them, from which they would soon depart.

Avenues for interstate traffic bounded the other two sides of the park, going toward the overpass loop and thruways that, like neckties in the hands of infants, had done strange things to every city, for nothing had been planned . . . The rush out of town, like the rush into town was something that happened in spite of purpose, in all the mess and noise it created.

So too the suburbs, the other end of the rush to and from, made the thirty, forty or fifty mile drive a thing to be forgotten, and it was. Like the visual barrage of billboards, like radio weather, in fact like the landscape itself. Who remembered — or cared about — how the entire area, as far as the eye could see — suffered. So as cars drove from superhighways onto marked turnoffs, they approached their homes in new and not-so-new real estate developments, some built back in the fantasy days of secluded isolation away from the city where they worked, where the air was cleaner, the water — ah yes, but, typical of fantasies, it all dissolved into used car lots, sagging wire fences, trash dumps, oil sumps, cheap national beer outlets, fast food, fast food and more fast food joints, gas stations, state liquor stores and the real proof of hi-tech, new computer world fantasy order: the busted up, rotting shacks and houses of the poor and homeless.

But back in town, across from CROSSOVER ACRES, and their pricey little park and its shopping strip, was a development of another kind. Backed up against the tall support columns under the overpass to the thruways, and a seeming future: in ash-dry dirt, scorched brown, tangled, crushed grass and weeds, garbage and trash below the vast skyways for racing machines: more homeless lived, among empty beer and soda cans, bottles, ripped clothing, pillow and mattress stuffing, shattered furniture, down on their flattened cardboard boxes, in outdoor bathrooms . . . the rear of one building faced this, except there were no windows, just a massive big-bricked wall-ended blank, in a very real aspect of tomorrow: rejected space, underneath and behind corporate expansion, going unnoticed, except to the historic desperate, who lived there.

Around in front it was state-bunker style architecture, all one storey high except for the main office building, which was two. Facing a sectioned parking lot and crabgrass lawn. Across from Crossover Acres — pale yellow brick, smoked glass windows, round corners.

The two-way avenue that extended as far as the eye could see — farther — east toward the desert and west toward the mountains (the suburbs extended north and south). In the outskirts, far away, at either end (of the avenue), the west end became a country road to the foothills marked by a run down motel and gas station. Out east on the desert, it joined an interstate heading north.

But on either side of this long, long east/west

thoroughfare, were in particular on the south side, tall, but sagging wire fences, on metal posts, with pieces of barbed wire. And behind this, an armada of spread out ruins of government machinery, on thousands of barren acres — all government property. Naked, half-finished foundations, isolate walls and corners of cinderblock buildings. Water wells just begun, ruined trucks, cars, bulldozers, road-graders, fractured chairs, hard-hats, clothes and tools, half sunk in dirt and sand. Sacks of cement torn, ripped open: rock hard. Torn sheets of plastic and paper, piles of auto and truck tires, scraps of paper, rolls of wire, and smashed lumber, lath, and shattered plaster in the gray and brown dust, and sand, looking like the landscape of a far away planet, no longer useful in an industrial galaxy.

Miles and miles of this vista, from the foothills of the mountains until the approach to the park, and that bunker across the avenue from it, with a large sign at the edge of the flagpole area, some sixty feet from the main entrance and the parking lot as well, where the Director, no longer called the Warden, parked his car. The sign was very different from the one in the park, bearing the names of the Governor, the Mayor, and a couple more state and city pals, in a language no longer of prisons, but of Corrections, at this Parkside site. The date it was built. Name of the architectural firm.

Monday, Wednesday and Friday, from one until three. I had a job teaching there.

I do it for a living.

Younger and older students, mixed races, co-ed. They'd bring their poetry — or other writings — to class, read them out loud, and we'd discuss it. All of us would. I didn't care what they wrote, as long as they brought it. I'd told my boss, a Mrs. Tracy, they've got to bring work. She said okay.

A local bookstore invited me. Jay Flattery, Prop. He carries a couple of my titles.

One of the clerks, a young white kid named Tad, was my chauffeur. He taught in the prison, too, and had had the same students, so he briefed me. But not much, except to talk about Sherry and Gina.

The prison was in truth a house of detention, meaning the population was transient, nobody would stay very long, two years tops, either to go farther out to the big maximum joints, or get out on bail or parole. And go home — if they had a home. If not, state/city halfway houses. They go out on work-release before they get parole, I should mention that. Not so simple as the media makes it: nobody knows except prisoners in process.

I'd never had a group, in these short jobs I do, of young and older, mixed race and co-eds, so I looked forward to it.

But I didn't look forward to going inside. I never do. Prison is the only experience in the world that gives two faces to concrete: outside looks different, inside the same.

And, typical, if not ordinary, I discovered everything later. The job of teaching poetry in prisons is one of working with individuals and their writing. The prison as such is unrelated because we get very involved in classes, and as we know — poets who teach as well as students — all kinds of things disappear in the focus on manuscripts, including prison, racism, even poor judgment, and because so much is spontaneous, I'm never quite clear what went on until afterwards, and it's too rare that I have someone to talk with who understands. So Tad and I hit it off right away, and after he picked me up that first day, that Monday, he saw I was in love, and he nodded, he knew about that, about Gina and Sherry, because he had fallen, too. Everybody did. He asked,

"Did you get a chance to read Sherry's journals?"

"No. Only heard what she read in class."

We were pulling out of the parking lot, onto the avenue that led back to the bookstore, where he wanted to go. It was that magic space of the day when the sun changes its mind and begins to go down, but is up there — right there — long enough to make it seem not so, and we thought we might like to have a couple of beers, and talk. Madge, my wife, was busy, so I was free. Sherry on my mind. Gina.

"Tough lady," he said.

"She's got so much personality she doesn't know which who goes where."

"That's right," he agreed. "I tried to break it down, to get her to express herself in poetry, and try using her imagination in short fiction — aside from her journals."

"Did it work?"

24

"No. She just keeps writing those books."

"Books plural?"

"Yeah. Over three."

"Boy," I breathed, as we rolled up to a red light, and stopped. "I'd sure like to see them!"

"Read those babies," he grinned. "Talking about digging gold, it's right there!"

"Say that again," I agreed. "Prisons overflow with talent."

The light turned green, he went into gear and we moved on, across an intersection. I told a couple of tales about talented convict writers. He was impressed.

"She's due to get out tomorrow," I said. Apologized. "Sherry."

"I knew who you meant." Paused. "Yeah." Paused. "Gina also knows."

True, but in retrospect, it seems more clear without making any more sense. The mass of people in prisons are so immature, they walk outside, blithe and happy, free at last. But the habit prison meanwhile became, with the nightmare of freedom too soon becoming its opposite, makes getting out of prison impossible, one of the true, cynical acts that can happen to a person. Like having a "great" job you hate or marrying for money: you make all the compromises, "it" makes none. So, Sherry got out of prison, but the next day nobody knew where she was. She hadn't a home or family to go to, so she went to one of the halfway houses, or was supposed to have, yet as Gina knew, and Mrs. Tracy, too, Sherry had gone to her boyfriend's house. He was a junkie. He was the reason she went to prison. If she wasn't where she was supposed to be, there was only one other place, the wrong one, meaning she would be discovered because she would not have reported in to her parole officer, and she'd be back inside, real soon.

So, all that gold Tad spoke of, in all her talent, was useless. Meaning she lied to me, in a wish to make her life better she had — like so many in prison schools — spoken a fib, a wish, saying she would be going to school in the fall, or spring . . . so I shouldn't say she lied. She relayed a dream through fantasy channels, as if it were real. And getting out of the habit of prison, she went right to her other habit, the second of the only two she had: him.

Her handwriting had been good: letters upright, formed — not slanted to the left or jagged, in fragments, or tailing away, thread-like. Blue ballpoint pen on lined pages of thick spiral notebooks. Three, over *three* of them! The fights she had with her mother, how she left home, wandered through back yards stealing food and — in the winter — clothing. Found in warmer weather a spot under a bridge in the park, near a water fountain — important, she had said — to be near a water fountain, yes. To quench her thirst but to also keep her body clean. She was a thoughtful writer. Had begun the passage with her telephone number at home, and knowing Jesus loved her, she was His little lamb, she'd be okay, you know, she wasn't going to die, but things got worse, she began to starve, and stole food from grocery stores terrified of being caught she phoned that number and asked her mom if she could come home and her mom said no.

End.

From her chair she looked up at me, eyes wet.

Wow.

I pointed to a fellow—a prisoner—in a chair by the blackboard, near the door.

"Comment?"

"Whaddya mean?"

"What did you think of what she read?"

"I don't know."

"You don't know?" I asked. "Did you like it?"

Murmurs round the room, unh huh, yeah. I did, so he said,

"Yeah. I liked it."

"Why?"

He looked at me. He didn't like this and he looked at me, shrugged his shoulders.

"It was good."

"I think so, too," I said. "How was it good?"

"It was honest," a woman's voice said.

The guy nodded. "It was honest."

"Good," I said. "But this is a Creative Writing class, so we're aware of the way work is written, as well as of what is being said."

He looked at me.

"I got that."

I pointed to the guy sitting behind him, under the posters on the wall for Black History, near a small bookcase of worn paperback novels.

"Comment?"

This kind of bullying I do cuts through a lot of unnecessary shit, so he, a little larger than the fella in front of him, shifted uneasy in his chair. Being called on to respond to a written work was . . . a new experience. Everybody in the room watching me, and him.

"I liked it," he murmured.

"Why?"

"Well," he licked his lips, and frowned.

"Let's hear it," I smiled.

"I liked it."

"Great, you?" to the young guy beside him (they didn't know each other).

"Well, you're asking me and I'm telling you I thought it was verrry interesting . . ."

"Me, too," I agreed. "Why?"

"She just said it, right on out."

"Yes," I said. Looking around the room with a smile. " 'She just said it, right on out,' " I repeated. "No nonsense. No apologies. No longwinded explanations."

"She said it right out," a slender black woman said, "because she's that way."

"That's right," another woman said.

"She writes like she talks," yet another woman said.

"Excuse me," a husky, male voice said, "but, when does this 'Creative Writing' stuff begin?"

"It has begun," I smiled, amused, which the others got, and snickered.

"This is it," a voice said.

"It has begun." Another.

28

"Oh," the fellow said, "um hum," he nodded, "I see." Held up a hand. "Go on." Paused. "Didn't mean to interrupt."

"No interruption at all," I said, in a different voice, to him, feeling a little music in me, his face crystalized — only so far, because it stopped, 'cause it was hidden behind it. These are not middleclass kids wanting a university degree, in these classrooms, these are individual lives far apart from each other, you and me, and almost all the world we know. They enter my classes in mask, sit in chairs and look at me, in a theater you have never been in, in a production of an Iron God, that you have never seen. He wasn't my age, yet he was older. People in prisons are older than old, and his eyes, as best they could, remained hidden. His skin was a smooth blend of black and dark brown. His body didn't move.

"None, at all," I said, again, because he had entered a more clear stratum, where people were talking about written words, and he as if woke up. I liked that, I loved it, it was happening to me, too, because it always happened, in verbal response, to written writing.

"Anything else, to add?" I asked the young man whom I had quoted. He was all smiles, chatting with a guy beside him.

"No — not unless you want it."

"I want it," I said, slow smile. He said,

"I sure don't like her mother."

Voices of agreement, naw, no way, unh *unh* among which my own:

"Me neither. Why?"

I knew what I wanted to say.

"Why?" Surprised. They asked. "Why?"

How dare I?

"There are two people in the story, talking," I explained, "about the writing. There are two people. Sherry and her mother, but there are three names."

"Jesus," a voice said.

I looked around, and unable to locate it, returned to him, who was puzzled.

"What do you mean?" he asked.

"Yeah!" a woman's voice.

"What *do* you mean!" Another's.

"I mean Sherry is a natural."

Sherry in hysterics—silent kind—with the woman I'd met called Angelina. Both laughing, Sherry hiding her face in her hands, kicking her feet and giggling. Angelina looking at me blushing in amusement, telling her to cool it.

"She doesn't bring anybody else in. She's a little lamb lost in the woods, with the cruel witch-mother, but Jesus will show her the way. Jesus becomes a maternal figure."

"Her mother?"

I turned to find the source, and saw a slender blonde, at a table to my right with other women, each with a small stack of books—textbooks—in front of them.

"I hadn't thought it so direct," I said. "But yes. She's done that in her writing, plus—ah but I'll wait."

I let everybody speak before I make a summary, but did admit,

"In doing this she's done what good, or, very artistic writers do."

"I am an artist!" Sherry cried.

"Can she draw? Hey! She can draw anything," a woman's voice said, and I turned to see a black woman, seated just inside the door, near the man by the blackboard.

"There you have it," I agreed. "She's an artist. Who writes like a writer." I stepped forward to the group, making a gesture of stressing a point.

"She doesn't bring anybody else in. And in this order, leaving the witch-mother, having mother Jesus show the way, she becomes a homeless thief, forced to phone home to her witch-mother who rejects her."

"And she gets arrested," said the husky voice, which I located, at a small table, in the middle of the room about ten feet in front of me. It had occurred to me, too, yet I felt a certain shock around the room, as others agreed.

"Excellent," I said. "So you see how she stops, in the anticipation of the obvious—"

"I wrote it in later," Sherry said.

"How much—"

"Here," she held up her notebook, having turned a page. "Right here." Pointing with a finger.

A couple of short paragraphs from where she ended.

I thought that was brilliant.

"She set it up."

They looked at me.

"I apologize," I said. "I listen with two ears: one

to the story, the other to how it's written, and as it would have been easy for her to read to the part where she was arrested, like most people would, she stopped, after she phoned her mother, and her mother said no, she couldn't come home."

Voices.

"Yeah."

"I think I get that."

"Me, too. But why?"

"Because to her," I said, looking down at her, and she up at me, eyes filled with questions, "it was over at the point where her mother said no, *not* where she got arrested."

"That's the beginning." The woman by the door.

I nodded.

"Like Mozart," holding my hand up. "As if there isn't an end, as if we write toward a constant beginning, which means in modern writing you," halting, "or I, we, write rather than toward just something, or somewhere, where it ends, we write toward a point where it feels complete, which is what Sherry did," gesturing to both, who were relative to the point: "before her arrest, which was her beginning, and," to the woman by the door who was watching me like a hawk, sitting back with a small smile, "stopping where her mother said no, which in this class, today, Sherry saw was complete."

"Where do you get that stuff?" Sherry asked, as the woman by the door put her arms on the table, and her face in her arms, laughing: whooooo*eee!* A couple others goggle-eyed. Some restless.

32

"I can't remember I heard such deep shit," someone said, "and I'm not sure I understand."

"That's not all I have to say, and," stepping forward to face the woman who said that, "it's you that makes me speak, not me. I wouldn't say these things without you. It has a name: dialogue. New ideas emerge from dialogue, which is what these workshops are for."

The man with the husky voice nodded.

"Any comment on Sherry's work?" I asked him.

"No. Not anything new," he added. "It's all been said here—"

"I have something, one more thing," I smiled. "But go ahead."

I liked it," he said, as if I hadn't said anything. "I thought it was honest. I know what she's talking about."

Yes.

The women in the room burst into agreement, all at once boy, *did* I—Yeah! Do *I* know what she's talking about!

"*I* do!"

A tall, white kid with brown hair who had a thoughtful, sad, anxious look—near tears—

"I got the same message from my mom this morning."

I wanted to be his dad forever—it happens fast here—hits hard. Voices:

"Aw shit," a woman's voice. "I heard that all my life. My mother—"

"My mother, my father, my fuckin' brother—"

"Aw yeah."

Amusement, anger.

And I let it go, until, on a feel of a round of repetitions I asked a half a dozen women, including Angelina (I'd not been introduced to her yet), what they thought about Sherry's journal entry. Each thought it was honest.

"How so?"

I looked around the room, not just at each person. In fact I walked across the room, towards the rear by the windows, beyond which the charming view of a, of the wall of a cell block, with grass too long, but, as I later thought, thank God they didn't cut the grass during my class: State lawn mowers blast, like helicopters.

I walked to the corner where a student was busy at a computer, beside a wall of textbooks, and said,

"We agree it's honest, and that we like it, but —"

"Her words are clear." A voice.

"Like she talks." Another. "I said that, to her. She's like that."

"But I don't know her," I said. "Do you?" to the others, everybody well almost everybody said no, they didn't either.

"Gina knows me," Sherry said.

Angelina — Gina — nodded, with a smile, and what a smile! She was a large, dark-haired, shy, full-bodied young woman, choppy hair round a heart-shaped face: direct but angled brown eyes, lips as soft and red as a baby's. Looking up at me, Gina pointed to Sherry, and placed her hand on her breast, said:

34

"We're best friends."

Sherry's face bright, and proud.

"Her words are clear," said the blonde at the table, with glasses on, rim no not rimless, round with steel rims. She looked intelligent, thoughtful and articulate.

"Excellent," I said. "Thank you."

She made a thin smile, but her words had sparked agreement in the others, as if a ball was passed from person to person, maybe the women in the room, in their green fatigues, as never seen on tv or in the movies, but a paradox of caution and a willingness to talk, or learn, to talk *and* learn as I have never witnessed in any school, anywhere. It was spontaneous, electric, how they shared in variation Sherry's experience with her mother, and agreed on its character of clarity, but also on its impact.

I agreed.

"Your writing doesn't need a lot of words, or extravagant, overblown descriptions, not that you write that way, but a lot of writers do. Over-description in beginning work indicates anger and insecurity, and none of it is needed. So much can be said in plain, clear language."

"But so much may not," said the husky voice.

I turned to him.

"That's true," I admitted, "because things are not always clear, simple, and —"

"Some things are complicated."

Everywhere I went he watched me, like the woman by the door — and others, too. I took advantage of that, by speaking to them with an intensity I reserved for my closest friends, thus giving them an instant identity, and after everyone had spoken, in response to what Sherry had written, I said (I made it brief) that while so much of the writing in prisons is of religious beliefs, Sherry used Jesus and the image of her being His little lamb in the way writers work, as a protecting image and transition point after she left, and she became homeless . . .

"I've read a lot of writing on Christian belief, in and out of context," I said, "but not as a means toward artistic completion."

"Why can't you just say, 'toward the end'?"

I located the voice: "This is a complete section of her Journal," I answered. "It stands alone."

"You use those words."

"I'm a writer."

"There you go," a voice said.

Amusement.

"To completion," I said. "Not 'The End.' This is fulfilling to her, not the end as a piece of string. This is why, in fact, she didn't read it through to the part where she was arrested."

"How do you know that?" Sherry.

"Tad told me."

Her face was older than her years, common in prisons, her features — but you didn't remember that, you remembered her personality. She was alive with character, and though unsure, self-conscious, ill-at-ease right away, vulnerable because no one had helped her learn, her face opened up, softened, and became happy.

36

"He *did?*" she beamed. "He talked — about *me?*"

"Yes. And what you had written."

She turned to Gina.

"They talked about *me!*"

"You deserve it," Gina said, raising her face, gazed up with warm, Renaissance eyes, and I was awed.

As if that wasn't enough, that I fell in love with them, but at the end of class, Sherry ran back to her cell and returned with some of her artwork. One which she and Gina had collaborated on. Gina wrote the text, a religious poem, and Sherry did the drawing . . . I get weary of religious writing.

"You've got to watch out for that. It's an illusion."

"What do you mean?"

"Religion is big league power. You know that. The same people who killed American Indians, who ruined Mexico, Central and South America, made slaves of those people."

They looked at me.

"You don't want to hear that," I said.

"We need to think it." Gina.

"I need to feel it." Sherry.

"Okay," I said. "It's part of your survival kit, but don't show it to me, because I know you can do better, and be more honest, writing and speaking about yourselves."

Well.

They saw I was angry, and they respected it, but they weren't going to shift positions, or adjust declarations because of it. You teach at Princeton, you don't learn this.

It was personal. True. Yet I determined I was going to say something, from the instant I heard her mention the little lamb, I made up my mind. Something clicked. I saw something and wasn't sure what it was, but religion was part of the illusion of life in prison, and I vowed to speak my mind.

It felt good.

Again, inside the classroom inside the joint, I didn't for fact quite know where I was, or to be honest, just what I was doing, but I sure knew who I was with, and, because I had learned it, the other half of the job was that *I* be honest—no matter what. I'm a writer not a teacher, so in that same face they're going to get a guy who's honest. It doesn't stop. It never stops. I show enthusiasm, and warmth—for example the man with the husky voice, whom I woke up one morning after, remembering.

The catalyst that broke discussion wide open, on the poem read by a young Latino woman—almost a girl. I sat up in bed, grabbed the pad of paper and pencil off my table, and began taking notes. As I did, I recalled his name: Clipper. Couldn't remember hers, yet the poem and its message was clear, something happened I could scarce believe, that told a story I'd not considered.

She had written the poem, and this is typical, she was not a poet, but had written this poem for this class.

She had gotten a letter from a guy in another

prison, a guy she knew, and the poem she wrote was to him in response to his letter, which she wrote for this class, not knowing anything about me. Mrs. Tracy had announced a poet coming in to lead some Creative Writing Classes, so the young lady wrote the poem, but before she read it, explained why, also explaining she had *written* why and would read that first. Everybody doing slow blinks. Furthermore, she said it was ten years ago.

"What was?" I asked.

"The poem."

"For this class."

"Yeah," she nodded, serious, with a frown: "I don't know if it's any good."

"We'll *see* about that," I teased, with my winning smile, it did not amuse her. But I make so many mistakes in my life I wasn't going to let one more matter, so I listened while she read the beginning after saying it was the beginning but not telling us where the beginning ended and her poem began, we were to figure it out, as she lowered her papers—three or four pages of blue-lined, ball point pen work—and looked around the room, at her audience. A clear story, that poem, a tale of woe. Teenage mother, bad childhood, so the murur-murmurs of agreement, general appreciation responses well taken, all were aware of her youth, profound appreciation. I pointed to the fellow by the blackboard, for comment, and he said it wasn't fair to judge a poem written by somebody so young. A lot of people in the room agreed.

I told myself to wait. See what they said.

"When did she write it?" Clipper asked her, turning in his chair, to look back.

"This morning."

"You wrote a poem that was ten years old this
morning?"

"Yeah."

I couldn't believe it.

He looked at me.

"It can take criticism," I said, looking around the
room, adding, "This was a poem you had memorized,
right?"

She nodded.

Dark eyes so big in her round, brown face, so
fixed on me, I felt alarm.

"Had memorized as a child, written as an adult.
This is a writing class, not a daycare center." Paused.
"We can discuss it for its message and the way it's
written."

They looked at me, each one, heads on a shelf.

I wanted to talk, but I contained myself, pointing to the woman next to the door, for comment.

"I liked it," she said.

"Why?"

"I think it's good."

"How about the way it's written?"

She looked at me, and it was clear what she was
thinking, so it took her a while to answer.

"I think it's all right."

"But could be better?"

"Yes."

"Good," I nodded, and to the group:

"We'll chalk this up to youth, and inexperience as a writer. This is pure expression, not literary achievement."

So I went round the room, as I do, asking everyone to speak their thoughts, in response to what she had read. And I said, agreeing with everyone — who could deny such an expression, felt as a child and written a decade later? She'd carried that around with her all those years — half her life! I was proud of her and said so.

"These honest statements are important to us, in more ways than we know. It clears our minds, lets us know how, and what we feel."

I crossed the room, and wrote on the blackboard:

EXPRESS YOURSELF. IT'S IMPORTANT TO KNOW WHAT YOU ARE FEELING. IF YOU KNOW WHAT YOU FEEL YOUR MIND IS CLEAR.

"And if in conflict with emotions, write them down, keep them separate. You can love someone but be very angry at them. Don't let yourself get confused: keep your emotions apart, and distinct, so you can know what they are. It may save your life!"

I looked at Clipper.

"Thank you."

"Why me?"

"You opened the door to discussion."

"Where did you get that?" Pointing to the blackboard.

"From experience. I'm a writer, not a teacher.

It's important."

"I do it, too," he said, opening a spiral notebook. "I write my thoughts."

"Great."

I walked toward him, as he looked down upon a page, with a note he had written, which upside down, looked like this:

"Date it," I said. "Day, month, year, and location. Very important. You can read this in the future, and locate your past."

"I ain't got no future."

"Everybody has a future."

Our eyes held.

"Everybody," I said.

"I don't know."

"He's been in and out of prisons all his life," someone said.

"That's true," he nodded.

"All right, that's the past. Begin, today, to date it, and write the location."

"What's the date?" he asked.

"The 5th," somebody said.

"May," he said, and he said the year.

"What's the name of this joint?" I asked.

Clipper told me, as he wrote it down. I said:

42

"This is your future."

He looked up, puzzled.

"Write your thoughts, express yourself today, you have something to read tomorrow."

He smiled, and put his hand out. General amusement, as we shook hands.

"Not bad," he grinned. "I'll remember that."

I smiled.

"You're my man," I said, putting my other hand out, and stepping closer, I placed it on his shoulder on impulse, contact, it happens fast — his shoulder was *hard*.

"A rock!" I exclaimed.

"I've had to be," he said, mixing the King's English with his ain't got no future.

That is what I took home: I had to touch him. The expression on his face as he grinned, "Not bad." His mouth had curled open in a grimace, revealing not only missing teeth but broken, split, brown stumps, and blood red gums. The skin on his face, layered over all his head, down on his neck, was the tissue that grows back over cuts, gashes and poundings. His face, head — and ears — were one solid bruised piece of bone and meat, of buried scars, welts, face as if a graft of scar-tissue, done with some mysterious artistry, not a line showed. Not one. All his life in and out of prisons — he had been beaten, whipped, cut, slashed, God knew what else, in the task of his life, plus the hands that held the whips, knives, guns, for a total abuse in childhood, in poverty, crime, streets, who knew — until the collision with the law, and the hand that held the club, and gun, that slammed the gavel down, and pronounced sentence, sending him into the hands of the prison guards, so outside and inside they beat him, and beat him. *They beat him and beat him and beat him some more, and yet again,* I couldn't stand it — looking at him. I wanted to bring him to me . . . the class was over so soon, as I left, walking down the corridor with Clipper — pausing outside the classroom to talk with Gina about Sherry, but at the door where I would leave, I shook hands with him, and said I'd see him again. He said good, he looked forward to it, I did, too . . . we poets, teach in prisons die not a little but a lot, it goes deep as we leave, and *leave them there.* As I left he thanked me, and his eyes met mine — his eyes, deep in the folds of his smooth face, had never left mine, for in prisons, you must always look into your student's eyes, so they can see you. Cops and guards avert their eyes, but creative prisoners know the eyes are the mirrors of the soul, seeing your soul they trust you. Clipper's big hand was smooth, soft, and warm in mine as we shook, and I went away leaving him there. His gaze deep, and dark, he — he turned like a shadow in that corridor.

I went away.

Yet they hadn't wrecked his ability to think. They'd battered but not killed his potential for sequential, inter-connected logic, yes. And as he sat in his desk and looked at me, dark eyes way back in under the smooth pulpy tissue, I had the sensation I was beholding a truer God than the one who ruled the

44

Christian world, in a vision of what it is to be human, and be alive, like the soul, a kind of soul we have to separate from our lives to comprehend, that this is the tortured spirit that stays alive, and drives the white man of the law with the club insane, in his homicidal jealousy.

This is the modern, hi-tech, Existential brutality that battered him within a fraction of his life, but not his talent, his gift of being able to think, and articulate. That's what he wrote, or had been writing, who knows for how long? This talented — potential philosopher, drawn to logic, deductive thinker: in these pages: he's Empirical.

They hammered, degraded, brutalized, shamed, humiliated and despised him, but not his ability to come to conclusions in logic. The thoughts — his thoughts, were jumbled, so too his writing. But the jewel was in there, as he made evident in class. Which was why I was compelled to go to him, for contact, being a different kind of man perhaps but in the way of him, and me, the same.

"Clipper," Tad murmured, looking in the rear view mirror, as he moved into the right hand lane — the turn ahead. "What a guy."

"I like him," I said.

"He's a survivor." Slowed, took the turn, shifted and the car gathered speed, toward the center of the city, and distant mountains. Nice. "He doesn't say much, but if he does we listen." Paused. "Be getting out soon."

"Depressing."

"His whole life is."

"He'll not stay out," I ventured.

"No."

"It's all he knows."

"Yes."

"How old you think he is?"

"Who knows? Forty?"

"His face is so walled in, he looks sixty." Chuckled. "And walks like a sphinx."

"Thinks like an Egyptian. He's been in and out all his life."

"I know."

"Age doesn't matter."

"That's true."

"Hell, he's older than the moon."

I smiled: "Spoken like a poet."

"I am a poet. I have an errand to run, can I drop you off at a bar I like?"

"Good bartender?"

"Yes."

"Great." Paused. "Rare these days."

He smiled.

Did what he said, pulled over to the curb and I got out. He gave easy directions, and drove away saying he'd see me in a little while, or so.

I enjoy walking sidewalks lined with trees that end at the foothills of mountains, so as I walked along, I was happy, yet thoughtful, and sad, plenty angry. Clipper, on my mind.

I hate prisons and the people who run them plus

the corporate police who run *them,* but I have to control my hatred, to do the job. But a tough control. Clipper was an accepted result of prison. He was everything a heavy, hi-tech computerized police state represents: the pure victim. Like Rodney King: the result of America's power play that evolved into a conformist machine process with no tomorrow. The computer was a today machine, like the media, and that day they began listing everybody in the country *on* the computer, our future dissolved into a consumer conformity and repetition. The poor people who because of their limits couldn't fit, broke laws so they could — fit, in the American Dream, an illusion of comfort through material possessions, except there was no comfort because the experience was ephemeral, the possession had no future because the goods were no good, and they went to prison for stealing them. Gene Debs was right: prisons were for the poor. And the computer-machines got serious about black men because white men — jealous white slaves, who called their trap freedom — were in control, the puppet masters pulled the strings, white fingers played the keys, and stared into the screen, at the growing list of arrests — and executions, and it was in this frame of mind, reacting to what had just happened in the prison, saying goodbye to Clipper, that I went in through an open doorway to a bar and stood there, and ordered a drink from a bartender I guess my age, on the plump side, bald on top, black hair around the sides, like Frank, back home.

Some young guys were at the end of the —

otherwise empty—bar, and the place was quiet.

"Yes sir," he smiled.

Italian. Dark eyes, broad face, smiling, looking right at me. I told him what I wanted and I watched him work.

"People used to go to bars because of the bartender," I said.

"That's right," he said. "They did."

He put a folded paper napkin on the bar in front of me and placed the drink on it. Placed another napkin behind that, and put a glass of water on it.

"But they don't anymore." Paused. "They don't know what a good bartender is."

I nodded.

"Shall I make a bill?"

"No, thanks," I said, and slid a five beside the chaser.

He nodded okay, rang it up and gave me change.

"Because they don't know what to drink," I said. "Or how to drink it."

He laughed.

"Marcello!" a voice behind a curtain called—a woman's voice.

"Ain't it the truth," he again smiled to me, raising a finger that he would be back, as he walked toward the voice who said his name again. The young guys looked up.

"Marcello, Marcello," they teased him. "You'd better get your ass back there . . ."

He laughed, and disappeared behind the curtain. I looked around.

The bar was about forty feet long, along the right wall inside the front door. Opposite, a doorway with a blue and olive block print curtains, that was the entrance to the restaurant. Both walls on the left, on each side of the entrance, were lined with glossy photos (signed) of local celebs. A framed newspaper review praised the food and wine list, giving it three stars. Near the cigarette machine up front, beside a (silent) juke box was a framed closeup of Jesus on the Cross, beside a Mickey Mouse calendar. Someone had drawn tits on him.

Kitchen in the rear, of a no frills, neighborhood place with a low tin ceiling, and one window in front with the name in blue neon.

The overall feel was a plastic shoe box with rounded corners. A semi-gloss tan ceiling and glossy yellow walls. Three or four young Italian guys were laborers, in denim wearing hard hats. Drinking tap beer and laughing about how little their boss's dick was. A mirror behind the bar in part reflected them, as well as sparkling bottles with silver pourers, on glass shelving, in tiers. The glassware had a glint, too, so too the beer taps, meaning the bartender was neat, and kept this place in order, giving it its warmth. Front door opened, a woman with three pubescent daughters entered, causing a stir among the guys, who cheered, applauded, and wisecracked as they rose, hugged the girls and their mom. I added water to my drink and sipped it. The mother went in through the curtains, and there was a lot of talking, to which the boys laughed, sudden feminine laughter, a man's, and everyone, to a secret joke. As the three girls stood outside, along the wall, blushing, the bartender came out chuckling, wiping his hands on a towel and began washing glasses, as two businessmen came in, sat at the bar, and ordered sandwiches and beer. Not paying attention I went into reverie, realizing religion was important in prisons because of something to believe in. Religion was their third source of nourishment, next to food and fantasy. But it was also an illusion. The belief in Jesus was a talisman that worked inside until they got out. Very primitive. But, weren't prisons also? Primitive?

The bartender had finished setting up the two men for their sandwiches, and was looking at me, causing me to remember . . . I forgot. I wear a small button on my jacket, above the heart, that says Teach Peace. I purchased it from a TWA stewardess on strike — remember TWA? — a few years back, at a union rally, one May Day. I forget I wear it, and was caught off guard, as the bartender asked, pointing —

"You one of them anti-war people?"

"My dad was in the Red Cross," I nodded. "In the First War. I follow him."

"Yeah?" Smile.

"Um hum."

"You weren't in the Second War?"

"No. Korea."

"Me, too." Paused. "Korea."

I looked at him, told him I'd been a non-combatant.

"Medic?"

50

"Yes."

"Excuse me."

I turned, to face a young man taller than I was, in a light gray suit with a pink silk shirt, open at the collar. He had a filter cigarette in one hand, and a bottle of Bud in the other. He put the filter in his mouth, and tilting his head to one side, pointed at my button, and asked,

"Why you teach peace?"

"I'm against war."

"Oh yeah?"

"I came in for a drink," I said, fixing my eyes on his. "Not to talk politics, or discuss personal opinions. I'll be gone soon, and you can—"

"You tellin' me what to do?"

"No. May I enjoy my drink?"

"What'll you do if I say no?"

I looked at him. Right at him. "I'm not afraid of you."

He was about to take the cigarette out of his mouth, and turned, to put the beer on the bar, as my shoulders relaxed. The bartender, Marcello, I realized, growled,

"He follows his father's footsteps."

Glanced down the bar. One of the other guys jumped up, walked toward us, grabbed the guy, spun him around, said:

"Shut the fuck *up*! Shut UP! He's having a drink. Let him *be*!"

My eyes were still on the bully's as he lowered his eyes. Just another softie, a tv-watching, beer-drinking junkfood jerk.

The second fellow said,

"Excuse us, excuse *him,* I mean."

But the other persisted:

"Where d'ya teach peace? Whaddya teach?."

"At the prison across from Crossover Acres. Creative writing."

"You *teach* in prison?" Marcello.

"Yes."

"You a writer?" Second guy.

"Teacher, he said," said Marcello.

"Where else d'ya teach?" asked the bully, who was getting interested.

"Wherever I can," I answered. "I'm a maverick. I do some academic jobs here and there, but, well, I'm a poet."

"A poet!" The bully.

They laughed, all, including Marcello.

"Why didn't you say so?" Bully.

"This nerd's *sister's* a poet!"

"I didn't know," I said, unamused. "How could I have?"

"I dunno," he replied, ashamed. But caught himself, and apologized:

"So I'm a fuckin' dummy. Here we got a real live guy poet, and we didn't even know it!"

Laughter.

"Marcello, buy this peace fuck a drink."

I made a civil expression of thanks, with a subtle no to Marcello, who concurred, and asked,

"You published any books?"

I nodded.

"I was just teasin' ya," bully apologised.

"He's a tease." Voice from down the bar. Amusement.

"Ask his wife," said the one who had come to get him, and as they walked in that direction, I heard another voice laugh, "Ask his wife." And they made mischief with that, raising beers to hide their expressions while they drank, as I sipped mine, angry.

"He's a good kid," Marcello said.

I nodded, and sighed, showed him a copy of my newest book of poems, which he glanced at, and walked to the end of the bar, and showed the group. They looked at it like benevolent savages, glancing at me. I was somebody different. That's why he'd bullied me. They asked how much it cost. I told them, also the name of the artist who did the cover. And the photographer who did the inside photo, of me. Like most men and women in prisons, they looked at it as an object, keeping their hands off it, yet touching it, it was alien, but I was, too. Marcello put on his reading glasses, took the book, and opening it, began to read as he walked back to the front of the bar, to stand across from me. He read the poem about the Panama invasion, and the bombing of poor people. I watched him read, line by line, to the bottom of the page, before he gave it back, looking at me in a new way.

"You like people. You're serious." He nodded. "Good."

I smiled.

He held up an empty glass as he raised his eye-brows. My glass was empty . . .

"Yes, please."

Door opened. Tad came in, stood beside me.

"Hi."

"Hi."

"One for him, too," I motioned. To Marcello.

The guys and girls at the end of the bar turned as Marcello's wife — I noticed — their mother, came out from the kitchen, to new amusement.

"What are you having?" Marcello, to Tad.

"Draft. Dark."

"Coming up." Paused. "You guys know each other?"

We nodded. He asked Tad:

"You a poet, too?"

"Yes."

Marcello smiled anew, in himself very amused, and as he made my drink, and drew Tad a cool glass, he asked,

"Do *you* publish?"

"In magazines."

"No books?"

"Not yet!" Tad — laughed, bending over.

"He will," I said.

"Thanks." Tad. "Stick around. I need you."

"Do you also teach in prisons?" Marcello, with some suspense.

Tad pointed at me: "With him."

We three chuckled.

"You against war?"

"One hundred percent."

"We're just a couple of peaceful poets," I explained. "Who came into this pleasant establishment for something cool, after a hard day's work behind the walls."

"Well," Marcello spread his hands, "it's good to see you. May I ask a question?"

We nodded.

"Why in prisons, why not in schools — ?"

"There's a lot of talent in prisons. Raw talent," I said.

"They're not spoiled, middle-class jerks, looking for a grade." Tad.

"And you like that?"

We looked at each other, nodding.

"But we learn, too." Tad smiled.

"You bet," I agreed.

"You don't learn anything teaching in college?"

"Sure," I agreed.

"Not what WE learn!" Tad exclaimed.

"Which is — ?" Marcello began, but his smile broadened, as if anticipating the answer, he was at one, with us —

"Reality, and —" I began.

"Freedom." Tad.

We raised and touched glasses, and toasted Marcello, next ourselves, in a tableau: sun coming in the front window, the three of us there at the bar . . .

"To freedom!"

WEDNESDAY WORSE

Because of highway construction, we came in from the southeast, on a different angle from the prison. Saw it crouched like a concrete bunker, its flank facing a wide intersection. A paradox, always, against the spectacle of the distant foothills, and majesty of the mountains, tall against the sky. They used to be snowcapped, as Tad said, and I knew, but due to global warming, no more. Driving up into them from the desert below, he said, there's a lot of dead timber, and for a mile or so, ratty, dry split pines, brown needles and undergrowth of bushes and smaller trees, crispy from auto/diesel exhaust. Big trucks.

From a military point of view, the prison could defend CROSSOVER ACRES — prison with troops and artillery — the newest model of totalitarian chic.

He dropped me off in the parking lot, across from the entrance, saying he'd see me later. I watched as he — sitting high behind the wheel — angled out into traffic.

I walked through tinted glass doors into a reception area like a square box with yellow walls, low, gray hung ceiling, and a darker gray, almost bare floor. But the yellow color wasn't from a mix of white and orange, but more white than orange with a drop of umber, so it had a pale, hidden appearance, and though the color was called Naples Yellow, on prison walls where it is popular, it has the effect of pale growing more pale, like a mood, disappearing. The gray on the ceiling panels had no blue, so it was the dead color from plain black and white, more toward the black, and its matte ugliness told, to a discerning eye, the reason why, just in the front door, the place was not for the living.

In the center of the plain floor, rows of about forty curved plastic chairs — all empty — faced a wall of tinted glass. All this was new, spotless.

All walls empty except for a framed bureaucratic diploma at eye level on the left wall (as you entered) that confirmed the name of the institution, the city it was in and the various names and titles of the local dignitaries proud to serve the public. Correction Facility of Incorrect Speech, Spelling, Grammar, and Thought.

The other wall featured doors to lavatories, a small block of wall lockers and, down near the end, where it met the wall of dark glass, was a dark brown door with a little sign that said Official. Shh. Secret, and — brown, for the word was secrecy, for the other, bigger word, Security, for the other, hidden word: retention, containing brown doors marked private, secret official, to slide, slip deeper in, to hide what was hidden inside: living bodies obeying orders to keep their secrets and us secure, so vital to our nation that they obey behind those brown doors, in there, hidden: hi-tech electronic power: armed, uniformed figures moved like shadows ahead of me — on a raised inner

58

platform—making them higher, to seem bigger, more powerful, so in getting my clearance I looked up at them behind the dark glass, at their featureless pale masks with eyeholes and mouthholes, while down below, beside a sign with instructions, a small, geometric slot, where tips of fingers took my photo ID that I slid in under, in a shallow cavity in steel, an ashtray shape. Pale fingertips passed me a Visitor's Pass Card with a clip, and a small, smooth brass coin about the size of a quarter. A voice told me to put my coat in a wall locker.

I obeyed. Crossed the floor to the wall lockers, taking off my jacket—removing things I needed— folded and placed it inside, closed the door, removed the key, crossed the floor and slid it in the steel place under the glass where fingertips took it, and I saw, placed it on top of my ID card, in line with other visitor's ID, arranged like cards in solitaire, near what looked like a red telephone. I recalled our favorite Attorney General Ed Meese, and the red phone on his desk, beside toy squadcars, sheriff's badges, and pistols, as a metallic voice said,

"Go to the door on your left and wait."

I obeyed. I went. I waited.

A buzzer sounded.

The door swung inward.

A woman stepped out fast, very close to me, her face up to mine, expectant, lips parted, as if emerging from a spiritual experience—eyes wide, face flushed: cried:

"*Here* you are!" Paused. "You *are* Francis Robinson?"

59

"Mrs. Tracy?"

"Yes! Me! Don't you remember? We met—"

"Yes, I do! I—" stammering, "but—"

"Are you cleared?"

"Yes. I'm right here!"

"Good, let's go, we're running late."

We went, inside. I closed the door, steel with a steel handle the size of a hammer's, the door closed as in a submarine, a thousand feet down, with a boom echo. Boom. I hastened to stay at the side of my escort. Our faces had been so close I hadn't recognized her, and as I walked with her down a short, narrow corridor toward a duplicate door, the pale yellow wall on my left and wall of tinted glass, shadows moving inside on my right, she, or we, waited for the buzzer to open the door. I was shaken because knowing who she was was making no difference from the other I hadn't known, who had surprised me, not so much as between two kinds of persons as it was of one real in memory and the other in a sudden unknown. I yet gathered myself, and we stood before the closed steel door. Dark gray with matte steel trim and handle. Buzzer rang, which startled me but not her, for she turned the handle, the door opened outward, and we entered what I realized was the central or main corridor.

She walked ahead of me while seeming at my side, as in part I saw her in profile even whilst she looked full at me . . . a high energy figure, talking fast, very intense, and distracted (who wouldn't be), by the complexities in the job, which is what she was talking about as we walked. Among a stream of inmates and guards walking to and fro, we neared classroom #4, on the left, getting closer. Across from windows on the opposite wall, which faced the outside, a perfect example of anal architecture, for retentive security which defined an insecure power: not thirty feet away stood a cube with an inset air vent, at the end of a sidewalk which began who knew where? Around the corner of another building? But in the area of the vent was a patch of dead grass, more wasted space. A mower wouldn't fit if grass grew, so who cared? Dead grass revealing the dry gray dirt of neglect: outside of prison reflecting the inside.

The door to the classroom faced, across the corridor, the window facing the vent. And—beyond—a clipped, trimmed, bureaucratic lawn, beyond which the extended parking lot, facing a wide boulevard, and the park in CROSSOVER ACRES. Prisons, in their vicious, self-conscious and vindictive ugliness, lurked on the edge of human reality, never at the center, even if at center they sat or sprawled like murderous bogs and swamps. This was true about the great malls, too, which explains how in part the country has lost its center: we have fallen into the illusion of the hub as swamp, without axle, cotter pins, spokes, and fulcrum. Without a center, swamp centers, on remote horizons.

Space, infinity have become empty, which we are free to ignore and pollute—don't worry. If we don't think about it, it won't bother us. This is the way that prison architecture has influenced the construction of elementary as well as high schools, colleges and universities, and you bet, corporations . . . the the shopping malls Americans flock to are constructed on the plan of prison cellblocks, with shops and restaurants on the left and right of a central corridor, not too removed, with the high security, of expensive condos, and hi-rises: the image of 21st Century America, with a computer God: He's a real clean religion, like video. You don't have to feel (or believe) anything.

Mrs. Tracy selected one of about fifty keys, while a guard watched, she opened the door to the classroom.

"Thank you," she said to him, as he nodded, and moved away. And we went inside, her body seemed to glow as she entered, and I followed, indeed the room itself seemed a residue of her whirl, her spirit, and in the combine — always, every day — of memory, intention, and determination, the room had a warmth and spirit . . . she moved toward her desk and the phone, carrying her non-stop monologue with every move she made, for she had other places to be, in the prison, other classrooms, other students, not to mention the prison officials, and their secret, monolithic security games, to make her impossible job twice so.

"There were billet inspections this morning," she explained, "and the students missed morning classes, *annnnd,*" glancing down a blurred xerox directory-sheet of numbers and secret codes, where classroom #4 was, among six vertical boxes with numbers above each box, one through six, and down the left, inside each box, were prisoner names, and the number of each billet they lived in. There were about fifteen names in each box. On the top, inside each box, was the number of the guard/information station for each billet. On the right side of each box, across from each student's name was their designated student number, and, as these were handed out every day (except weekends, although special classes were held on weekends), the number — one through six — of each classroom they could attend that day.

I'd been through this before, but not quite such compulsive details, although I knew the people who ran the prisons hated, loathed and despised anybody coming in they thought might be a security risk, meaning any hint of education or rehab Lordy Lordy, the sky is falling, so they made it very near impossible for the students, and double that for directors like Tracy. But in her determination, she kept on, which the classroom reflected. Her desk, more a surface for the proof-on-paper how stupid, useless and non-functional prisons were, with stacks of blurrred, faded, and crooked, off-the-page xerox copies of rules, regulations and orders, new designations, codes, numbers, titles, and names that changed every day, plus pads of paper, pencils, erasers, and . . . numerous magazines relative to that dreary place, that people where- how- whyever had given her, and not knowing what to do, she put them on top of the others on her desk. The desk of national perpetual motion, here but over there, there but elsewhere, and there, somewhere on the way to another place Hi! where? Here, reflected society, too. Not just architecture. Military. Post office. Welfare.

A computer behind a makeshift partition in the right hand corner, to the right, across the floor from her desk. In fact there were a couple of chairs loaded with books, magazines and more papers, there beside and against her desk, and as it, her desk, was just inside the door, as we entered, I had to step around it, to get to where I would be, to face the students. A table, a small, wooden table not so scarred as others I'd seen, stood as if waiting. I'd used it last class, so today I took my books and papers out, pad and ballpoint pen, realizing as I had before, I had very little room, between the paper mountain (of her desk) on my left, and the computer corner to my right, where two students crouched, as if avoiding gunfire, eyes glued to the screen, in the pose computer addicts so enjoy: peering into the screen as if it held answers, hey! was there a future? Maybe life had meaning! Clickety-click went the skeletal, electronic keys, which, gazing at the magic screen they didn't hear: had made them deaf. No, blind.

I moved the table a few feet out into the room, while Tracy was on the phone, she stood, back to me, in a stacked niche flat against the wall all the way behind the door, on top of a bookcase jammed with textbooks and papers . . . not just a telephone, but an inter-security machine with about ten keys: out of the corner of my eye, I saw her hitting the keys, while I adjusted the table, my own things, and thought

64

about rearranging the chairs where students would sit. The door opened and two or three in fatigues came in, looked at me, sat down. I never knew. This had seemed a sort of study-space, and also reading room. I, the intruder.

We were running late. Yes. But!

On the wall just to the left of the door as they entered, blackboard, with chalk and eraser! Always made me happy. Beyond, along that wall, and continuing around the walls of the room were posters on Black History Month, Women's Rights, blow-ups of posters of the U.S. Constitution with a message underneath, samples of student work, samples of proper grammar, and stuff a little like educational TV, in primary, popsicle oranges, cherry reds, sky blues, etc. In the corner on a direct angle opposite the door was another little nook, like the computer's, where a mobile bookcase, on an angle, made a partition. Behind it a small table, a desk and a chair, where a young woman sat, reading a book. She had been there, like the computer fiends, since we entered (and would remain, through my class). Maybe they lived there. I didn't know where to stand. The room wasn't very large, seemed too many chairs, and, not uncommon in prisons, all out of place, with the chairs facing her paper desk mountain. There was a table, big enough to be a desk, out in the room in front of the blackboard. But students sat not at that table but out from it, facing Tracy's desk, and . . . as I pondered my place in the arrangement, the door opened, and at first two, followed by a couple of other students I recognized, came in, chose seats, sat down and began opening notebooks, taking out papers and talking among themselves while watching me, the way they have in being awkward, self-conscious, because I'm new to them.

This is what Mrs. Tracy was on the phone about or, who, rather, all her calls were for . . .

"Hello? This is Mrs. Tracy, calling from classroom number four. I'm looking for prisoner Fernandez." Pause. "This is A-Billet isn't it? Yes, I thought so. Well, his number today is D-2, could you, yes, I'll hold." Pause. "No? Do you know where he is? Listen, his designated number yesterday was B-2, Fernandez. Ramon. What do you mean he's gone? I saw him yesterday, and he said he'd be in class today . . . No. B-2, no, that was yesterday, today it's D-2. He's not there? Hey, hold on. Could you check Cooper, Brown, Rodriguez, D-4, D-6 and D-9 . . .? Yes, they're from A-Billet. Yes. I'll hold." Pause. "Yes. Rodriguez, Cooper, Brown."

More students came in.

I crossed to her — she'd been on the phone going on ten minutes, phoning in search of students, to "call them down," on the computerized system, while the students she was looking for entered the room.

Startled but confused by what was going on. They came because there was a class. There were different classes in this room all day long, like in the other classrooms. The guards in the billet, on station, forced to read the secret, security-coded sheets, but because there had been an inspection, the prisoners who were students departed right after, and, although most were late, they had come right down, and the guards, who had gone their rounds inspecting, didn't know where the prisoners were, only that they weren't there, forcing guards to recall the coded numbers inmates were given the day before, and Mrs. Tracy had learned that, and used it. I was at her side as she spoke, and heard guards remembering . . . oh yeah, yesterday he was D-1, etc.

She turned to me, not one bit disgusted, and seeing the students, expressed pleasure they were there. Didn't say she'd been looking for them, only—

"Here you are!"

All smiles.

"Plenty of paper?" she asked.

Yes, Mrs. Tracy. Unh huh.

"Ballpoint pens?"

Unh huh.

And to me: "If they need anything," opening top middle desk drawer, "it's here. They can help themselves."

I saw pads of lined yellow paper and a packet of ballpoint pens, on top of countless other objects, not paper clips or rubber bands. Security. A paper clip could be made into a weapon. True. So could a personality.

The experience of teaching in prisons has to be read in part like an essay, because of the unfairness, the brute indifference, cruelty and casual manner in the way we who teach are treated along with the prisoners. Women writers and poets in particular. I must say, speaking for my *compadres* nationwide, that I teach as a writer, not as an academic or public school teacher or, as a do-good liberal.

"It's great you've come," Mrs. Tracy smiled, gesturing to the room, where about twelve or fifteen students sat, in desks, looking at her, at me and at their papers.

"It's great to be here," I responded.

"They talked about the last class," she said, in a way of making reference to "they" and "them" as hers, except that very "they" and "them" it meant their recognition as a group of students was assumed, and would be responsible to their individual identity: she made them proud to be there: one by one in a group, was individual. Me too, in a special grace, in their trust, because they were, in their individual, and group way, the most vulnerable students a teacher could face, because of their expectancy, and the durable, even transcendent trust they placed in me, given them by Mrs. Tracy. It was and it is, will always be, to be, to me, that which is magnificent in the arts, and the reason the arts should function in society for the people, not for an educated, academic snob elite. Because the arts belong with people because poetry and music, dancing and painting, like carpentry, and the knowledge of the trades, are as direct a part of life as — life itself. Plumbing, electrical work, construction work, painting and writing are elements of the life of all people, in our talented, once in a while genius-gifted population: art is understanding understood through creative works that transform what can be into what will

68

be in a constant flow, to every individual sense including the intuitive, through all our lives: implicit in the orange in the orange: the beta in the carrotene.

"Did anyone bring any writing?" I asked.

"I have a letter my husband wrote me," announced the short black woman — sat by the blackboard last class, today in a chair beside the chairs stacked with papers and magazines by Mrs. Tracy's desk, Mrs. Tracy who had waved goodbye and departed. Gina looked up at me.

"Her husband's in federal prison."

Other women nodded. Yeah. Unh huh. True.

"That's right," the woman nodded. "We keep in touch, with letters."

"Good," I said.

"But I don't know if I should read it, it's . . . personal." Big grin. Others laughed.

"You mean it's juicy?" asked a young black fellow across the room, whom I hadn't seen before. Not here, but on the streets, yes. Lots of him: face/body crisscrossed in conflict: he didn't know how to be, and being a cynic, was cynical. Very sad, triple that in anger.

"Naw, it ain't juicy," she said, "it's more . . . well I don't know how to describe it, but to me it's beautiful."

I liked it. I was getting interested. One of the women said,

"Why don't you read it to us?"

The blonde, with glasses, prim look, and three or four textbooks on the table in front of her, a spiral

69

notebook to go with each. I have no idea what she was in for. I never ask. It's none of my business. Assume drugs.

I nodded. "Please."

Most everyone had gotten settled, as the black woman took the letter from the envelope, unfolded it, and began to read. Her voice was strong, but husky,

"Nice and clear," I said. "Loud, so we can all hear."

Her head tilted down to face the letter, she raised her eyes to look at me, low smile, nodded:

"I ain't used to this."

Amusement.

I had stepped into the center of the room, but fearing I might block someone's view, I crossed, to stand near the blonde by the wall — opposite the blackboard.

She began to read:

The rhyme patterns in prison poetry — for the letter she read was a poem — are familiar to all who know prison writing, that of Hallmark greeting cards: simplistic, of four lines, where the last word of every second line or so rhymes, in a confessional-frustrated-angry-loneliness tone with rhymes like cell and hell and jail with bail . . .

About twenty stanzas in all — twenty! — and around the seventh or eighth, after he had fun telling her of his love (from above), for her, he was, it was clear, thinking in words, so what he was feeling was what he was dealing, and it began to be clear right here she was getting out of prison before he was, everybody in the room began to focus a little sharper, seeing her at home and him still in the federal pen — implications *all kinds* of implications — he knew she would still be his, because that's the way she is, and the way *he* is, too, but blue, with her, except she'll be free, see and he be all locked up in stir, and things settled down to the obvious, as he expressed how he wanted his arms around her, like a sudden, unexpected jolt as a train stops he didn't *say* Cupid, but began talking about that little baby with the bow and arrows, how those arrows had been let loose on them both, that's what had done it, six or seven stanzas on that had us all gaping, not knowing if we should laugh or cry, the same with her. She read it as if she had never seen it, so moved and amused, but a little frightened, too, and anxious, as he fought a wild accusatory rhyme battle with Cupid, verbalized through his wife that was, like the song, easy enough to say but impossible to play, so as he ended up expressing his loneliness in his cell in this hell, missing her, he'll love her forever, wherever . . . she was, even alone, at home.

But the impact on her, an impact on us all, so as people reacted, amused, thoughtful, confused, uneasy, a few — including me — applauded, I could see — we all could: everybody in the room saw how undone she was, which she covered with aloof amusement in a warm expression, as a couple of the women looked at me, wanting to talk, I nodded and gestured to a woman near me to begin, and from her went around the room, finishing up with the person nearest the door, but maybe for a first, I didn't do my usual summing up, because it had been said by us all, at that point, and the eagerness — the uniform acceptance of this 100% prison poem with its attack on Cupid, caused such complete acceptance, yet for different reasons, with most everyone (including me) in awe, and a little cautious to go overboard in any deep response, because the woman who read it was so shaken — in the end it was she, who did the summary. I had something to say, but in deference to the range of emotions she was going through, I remained silent. Although, in truth, it was so obvious what I had to say, I was sure everybody knew . . . well, no matter.

The dominant response was that he was very much in love with her, to which she reacted with fervor, aw yeah, *very* much in love with him.

"He's unhappy I'm getting out before him," she added.

Which was clear, but *she* wanted to say it, to general agreement, understanding and sympathy: she too was unhappy.

The next most popular response was to Cupid, universal amusement and respect. *Everybody* — most of these students didn't know each other — spontaneous, me, too, agreed. Cupid was the son of either Mars or Mercury and Venus, also called *Amor,* symbolic of love, to show how deep the antiquities are in our culture, I was very aware of the paradox her husband had created out there, in the federal pen in blaming the image of love, or love itself, for the love he felt for her. He was angry and, it was clear, happy and — also — amused, at what he was writing because he was saying something he wanted to, and in that not-so-simple conflict, rather than blame himself, and her, for their love, he blamed love, throwing everybody in the room for a loop. So while we heard and agreed, it was only possible to undertand a little, because there was so much — it was defined by its tone: his sense of humor, his sudden artistic imagination, his anger and — her, *her* feelings, all made it a difficult success, but that was by no means the end of it, because everyone in the room knew what it was about, and in some variety what she was feeling, so, while written to her, it belonged to us, yet that, *that* was not the end, either, and in response to it, these things were to a certain point spoken, except where nobody, including me, wanted to admit how, in each of our lives, *and why,* we agreed, because that was, that *was* personal, well maybe but! *maybe too* personal.

It was a discussion on levels where we kept seeing the same thing — a montage — through it, not one of adding new insights, new revelations, it got more complex as it continued because it could only end up where it began: a poem to her, became, in the end, a poem to her, and having heard the poem, we looked to her. Everybody. Looked to her. All of us.

Looking at her.

No matter what we thought or felt, the poem was to her, therefore hers, and we were pretty sure we knew how she was reacting to it, but nobody, including me, wanted to say it because everybody was, in a sense, in her place . . . She was getting out before he was. He was stuck inside, and she was going free. I don't think it was about fidelity—nothing in the poem touched it, and he would have said so, had he thought so. But, you see, he was *in*, and she would be *out*: that defined it, and he blamed love for letting her out, he was stuck inside with it without her.

So at the end of the discussion—kept alive by my getting people to talk about what they felt, that they liked it yes, but why, and how as well—at the end there was a kind of spiritual quiet, as we looked at her, sitting in her desk with his letter in his hands, everyone outside her, around her, feeling what she was feeling but letting her be alone in hers.

In a prison that was a detention center, everyone was getting out, they knew their dates, that's all they thought of. But—hear this—in respect and their empathy, they didn't ask her where, and when, he would go free. This was not Yale.

Gina needed glasses. I'd noticed it right away, during the first class, as she held a page from Sherry's journal, to read up close, her face buried in it.

"You need glasses."

"Yes," she nodded. "With luck I'll have them before I get out."

So she read something she'd written for this class and . . . I don't remember what it was, because I remember her, who could not? She had an indelible effect, and looking at her, watching her in that room, I was amused but so in love I allowed myself a mere hint of a smile. She, pacing back and forth reading

74

aloud, face buried in each page . . . she turned to a next page with a motion we use to remove and peer into a hat. For she had written on lined paper, on a pad, and continued from the top of the other side: at first, in turning the page like a book it was upside down, and while correcting it, was surprised it was wrong, forgot what she was reading, and had to go back . . .

I had a conversation with her after class that because — once again — of her I forgot, but not all, yet I remember her in every way I'm able. One of the great mysteries in life is the mythic, not rare, beautiful in many ways, and all plain to see, and witness — in women in prison, but Gina was of all, the one. In being just herself she was deep, profound, mysterious and compelling, warm and giving, at once open and yielding yet closed and secret: the opposites in procreation, closer to a living goddess, more near the sublime, and face to face in the corridor with her, I saw in her expression and stature a feeling for life I had never seen in anyone before, nor had I expected to — the reverie known only through an a priori feel, which I experienced once, as a boy not more than five, alone on a beach, gazing out at the Atlantic Ocean. I call this my Atlantic Memory, infinity: intuitive reflections in the girl in the young woman looking at me, the reflective boy in a man growing old, in the vast crystal of existence, I'd met the actual beauty, her, in an actual encounter out on a corner of the edge, in a single swirl.

The paintings and sculpture we see of her,

walking—some of them—out of the ocean toward us—on the walls in the great museums and galleries of the world: she is naked, with small feet, slender ankles, long legs, a high, full waist, small breasts, long copper hair, oval face and neck set in the V between her strong shoulders, gentle arms and china hands with dimpled fingers. Her gaze is direct, expectant yet removed, in an unseen shadow she looks right *at* you, all around her, are curiosity, kindness, strength, and an open, eternal patience, she is closed and alone, content. Secret. Self-conscious in her youth she broke my heart. Living, full of life, I wanted to cry out—stay! Let's keep talking! So I—but no. She has to go because she is on her way, no matter me nay, unfair and untrue. I matter because I took her hand, I spoke with her, and we gave each other a big hug goodbye. And I'll say, one day, that I met a woman—two, in truth, counting Sherry—with whom I spoke: but one I had known from the beginning.

She walked away, yes. She turned, after we shook hands that last day, and walked away down that corridor outside the classroom, and I watched her in a suspense I'd seldom felt.

"So this is what goes on here," the fellow said, whom I'd noticed before.

We turned, to see.

"People bring stuff in and read it, huh?"

I nodded. While Gina had read, I'd noticed him writing, head down, expression intent, writing fast as he could, hand back and forth, I thought, because it's common enough, prisoners come in to my classes, and seeing writing, often sit in the rear, I suspect at ease in a group of people with a focus on writing, and do their homework for other classes, even write assignments, themes, etc. So I thought he'd done that, too. I asked,

"You've written something, for another class?"

"No!" Angry. "For *this* one!"

"Did you hear what Gina wrote!"

"No," getting angrier, put a hand out, "I know I should have. I know it. But I had to write this, see? Had to, right here."

"Okay," I said, "do you want to read it?"

"I don't know if I should. It's pretty violent and the language ain't very nice. It's . . . the straight shit."

The look in his eyes, of the hate we see in homeless black men, helpless, frustrated — pattern of self-contempt and hopelessness, begging for money but so angry they get very little because they frighten the people who want to give. Like me. Didn't happen often, but it did happen. Dark skin, dark eyes, whites not white, brown stained, bad teeth, unshaven. Slender. With that hollow-chest, so common to the homeless (men and women), rather an angular face than round. Short, kinky hair, not cut in the street fashion, he would be described by educated, insecure liberals and rightwing judges as having a bad attitude.

It was a new-universe face, and if we would want to get detailed in the description, behind the anger, resentment, paranoia, frustration and — grief — in his eyes, there was also terror, because while he knew who he was, nobody else did, or cared, except him, but the odds were so monstrous, in such steady brutality, he too had begun to believe he didn't matter: he was nobody even to himself. He is the potential everyone. *This is* the 21st Century Everyman. Nobody in the classroom knew him. Who was he? Where did he come from — ah yes, yesterday's sociological queries regarding the danger of mass conformity deepen the existential crisis of today: millions of lost, faceless human bodies, displaced in poverty and prisons: *who cared?* So, he read what he had written, sitting there in those clothes — you, hey, you know, you've seen the dirty t-shirt, vague, rumpled state-issue slacks, and the dreaded sneaker: more American symbolism. No socks: hands naked, flattened the paper on the table beside him, and leaned over it, hands flat, tips of fingers touching its edges, as he gazed, or stared, down at it, his voice harsh, nervous, tense, scared. His handwriting looked ragged and scrawled, yet people in prison who wrote only signs and symbols for words, read 'em like the King's English, and so did he, the first word, from the first word on no doubt about what he was saying. And he didn't blame Cupid, he blamed *women,* in a string of four letter words he just let go. Ripped away the curtain, exploded — it was her fault, *all* her fault, hers, *she* was to blame for his misery, failure, worthlessness, and for their children *she* was to blame, in one nonstop torrent, with at the end some references I didn't get, to his, was it her, parents? And his father because he didn't have a father, his father had gone — his voice, having hit a high level of intensity, stayed there, uncoiling out of his fury until he was finished, raised his head and looked around, in rare, apprehensive terror, and rage, until his eyes landed on mine, while nobody said anything, he didn't either, until the woman who read the Cupid poem said, in a clear voice:

"It's important you said that."

The blonde, with glasses — oh, don't appearances fool us! — said,

"Yes. I agree."

"A lot of men feel that way," I agreed, "and I wish more would say it."

But I was in shock, the kind where my own words made me self-conscious, because I didn't know what to say, how to frame what I was feeling. Until Clipper joined in, he too, agreed. He thought it was honest. Where was I? In the highest echelons of therapy, this kind of expression, revealing so much so fast, was stuff in textbook case histories, not living human beings, but it *was* in living humans — right here, in this classroom, it happened, and, listen! *Everybody understood, everybody congratulated him!* He couldn't believe it — neither could I but I did! And so did he!

But he didn't know how to show it. His face was too wrecked, so bitter, hostile, angry, sad, isolated and self-despising he couldn't show his happiness, and warmth: these people understood what he'd written, what he'd said, what he was feeling *and nobody hated him!* Dare he smile? Yes. He did.

He smiled. A beauty — whole face transformed.

Had he not been so blocked he would have wept,

but he didn't. He smiled, looking around the room.

"If you think about making that longer," I suggested, "give it more details, and background. Tell us who the people are you're talking about."

Voices round the room agreed, as we encouraged him to continue . . .

Several weeks later I realized what had happened.

Writing classes in prisons are open. They're unexpected free zones. Often rather lost spirits, children if you will, wander in, and so had he, to in this case witness a poem from federal prison, plus what Gina had read, walking back and forth, peering at her paper close up . . . it occurred to him — presto! It occurred to him he had something to say, so he wrote it down. *Bam*.

But surrounded by hopelessness and hatred, he retained the historical integrity of the nomad, the wanderer, who walked across the deserts, mountains, canyons and icy glaciers, for the full span of human history, and this lone survivor had come into my class, sat down and written what it occurred to him to write, and *read* it to us!

I stopped on the corner, looked up at the streetlight. Red.

I looked out at the sky, in that part of the city where I live, by the freight yards of yesterday's railroads. Tracks stretched to the horizon. The city skyline behind me, the light turned green, and, after having stopped at the farmer's market, I walked home under a high sun, thinking about him, how lucky

I'd been, to have this historic visitor.

Watching a young man shuffle papers nearby, I turned, looked at him. Our eyes met.

"Do you have something?"

He nodded.

"That's the paper he read last week, it got a 95 from the teacher."

"Ninety-five?" I asked. "Not 100?"

"No. She don't give out hundreds."

Amusement.

"It's good," she said.

"It is," another voice.

I heard murmurs and monosyllables of agreement. Looked at Clipper. His face impassive, eyes back at me like a face inside a tree, as I smiled, although he did not. I turned, and crossing the room to stand by the door, and the great sculpture of Mrs. Tracy's environment desk, while the young man read an essay that he'd submitted to another class, and gotten a top grade, concerning street gangs, which gave boys the opportunity to gain power in their identity by becoming the baddest of the bad, with the added perception that these gangs have replaced the family. I was very impressed, the classroom discussion was lengthy, and good. I learned a lot, and forgot not what he said, in that overwritten, non-artistic way of stating it right out.

Women in these workshops bring a different comprehension and response, and to his essay there was a general warmth because gangs were understood, part of life, all agreed it was too bad, but, in the classroom it was understood that they, the gangs, were their own world. Boys belonged to gangs. A boy—this boy— wrote about it, in prison, yes, we understand, but to have young women right there alongside, listening, gave it new dimension.

With women in the room listening and responding it had a fullness and depth that made it memorable, so that weeks and months later, seeing talk shows and interviews I recalled the young man's essay, how good it was and how moved the women had been. Well, it was indeed a Big One: gangs offering such identity through violence, and replacing the family as part of childhood. Wow.

A voice across the room caused me to turn, to see a young man speaking with a clarity and tone I wasn't used to, not in this context, more fitting at Harvard, I should say, but he said what the fellow had written was true, that he had been in gangs himself, and there was no doubt about the impact on teenage life. Too many boys never made it out of the neighborhood, or the gangs, and too many died not even trying. He had been in (high) school, and was doing well, but had dropped out to join a gang. General discussion followed, which I allowed, and—in the class before, I forgot to mention, while I wrote about Clipper, it had featured two, not just one, but two, interesting memoirs from childhood by two women, one of whom was so striking, with her pale, Garbo humility, and sadness, I felt trapped in how to respond, in— well, she blocked me to her writing . . . as in writing about prison writing classes one is compelled, even driven to write about the prison, there is a point of humility and empathy where expression falls silent. I didn't know what to say, and though I used words to cover for it, and the words were good, and had effect, they substituted for a desire to cross the room, kneel beside her, and say: "What can I do? Tell me! Please! How can I make you happy?" The wish, or hope for happiness and freedom for women in prison transcends the walls, and touches—as these things do, which is why teaching in prisons is a transcendent experience—undeclared feelings shared by all, all this not easy to articulate, but it has something to do with a universal world most of us don't want to be bothered with. So, where prison is an extension of an already miserable life, is on a varying selection of memories from childhood, another reason why they're often so childlike as adults or, as adult as they have become. Can be. Girls mature faster than boys because of the obvious, but in themselves, with exceptions, there's a closeness to the past that holds a potential chance for a real future. Both the memoirs that were read reflected this, as well as the depth of their feeling. The one woman, whom I wanted to kneel down before, had to pause at passages, lest she be overcome. Oh, baby, I thought . . .

The other was on going camping—overnight, where in discussion, after it was read, to our intense amusement, the author confessed she had gone with her boyfriend who, after pressure from the ladies, some blushing and wringing of hands—causing more laughter—she admitted he was the guy she married.

"Why didn't you write *that*?" Gina cried.

"YEAH!" Sherry.

"I wanted to," the author confessed, eyes wide, staring out from her little tent in the woods, into the fire . . .

"But that would be too much," I said.

Silence.

"Yeah."

"Aw yeah."

"Too much."

"Unh huh."

"That's right."

"Too much to ask."

Their voices all too soon became female sounds, as the room — ah, the women — reflected upon it in agreement, soon all were talking to anyone who would listen, what happened that day or afternoon or night they went camping, with their boyfriends, until that educated voice from the young man across the room — he wasn't much over twenty, sounded paternal, even wise, but likewise reflective, and sad, telling another universal story:

"I'm glad to hear this, but I have to say it never happened to me. I didn't go on any camping trips, any-where. I never left the neighborhood. I was on the street, it's where I lived, except at home, but my father was a drug dealer and alcoholic, so his clients were passed out all over the furniture, and my mother, well," he paused. "I'll tell you the day I get out of here, I'm not going back to that."

84

So, in this class, in his letting us know the essay on street gangs was authentic, he said, again,

"I get out of here, I am *not* going back!"

"What will you do?"

"I've a few ideas."

"But how about your family — your mother, is she okay?"

"She's okay," he said.

"Will you write about it?" I asked.

He looked at me, head a little turned away, gave me a sidelong look:

"About what?"

"That."

He thought about it. Good looking — too controlled but so it must, yes Lord, so it must be, all that rage . . .

"Okay. I will," he said. "For the next class?"

"Yes. Friday."

As I left the classroom I said goodbye to Gina — Sherry had gone free, remember, and nobody knew where she was, still. I walked away with Clifford, before I shook his hand, and that of the young man, who'd gotten 95 on his streetgang essay, as well as that of the other young fellow, who had agreed to write something for the group the day after tomorrow. The rest disappeared, as they do.

That night I had a dream.

I walked into an empty, but very familiar room, to see a man in a chair with his face averted. The room was so like a stage set, yet with the authenticity of a room in a story, in fact in Robert Louis Stevenson's great one, concerning a man named Markheim, who, on Christmas Eve, meets himself in an apartment behind a shop after killing the shopkeeper. There were a couple of walls of books, a closet door and curtains, a window through which I saw a sunny street and a lawn strewn with leaves, from overhanging branches of trees that came right to the glass. An oriental rug on the floor, a desk in a corner with a chair, and dictionary on a revolving stand beside a world globe in its stand. A light with shaded tassels hung from the ceiling, but it was off, for the sunshine coming in the window.

I entered the room, closed the door behind me, at least the door I had opened to enter, although not knowing where I had come from, and I walked toward the figure, hearing Frankie Laine singing *Black and Blue,* I paused, as the figure turned toward me, and I saw a man, a man my age, way overweight, it — it was my closest childhood friend, who had died some years back. Heart failure. I had been stricken for we had a falling out over Vietnam and after many years had renewed our friendship. I was overjoyed.

"Lloyd!" I cried.

He looked at me and smiled the way he had as a boy. I was very near tears, and again said his name —

"Lloyd," pleading with him . . . "Are you okay?"

But he was silent. His eyes grew dark, and he began, he began to disappear, but before he altogether did he turned away, so I last saw him with his face

averted, before I, I became aware the room was empty, the chair in which he sat, also, even the sun and
trees, and leaves outside seemed still, as if missing him,
for of a sudden the world was silent, and nothing, as
if poised toward an unknown change, nothing moved.

Driving away from the prison, along the boundary of
the park, the wind had risen, and from behind the
mountains clouds appeared, coming toward us, getting darker as they came.

"Looks like rain," I observed.

"Sure does."

But, in the caprice of mountain weather, not just
rain. The top layer of clouds — white and billowy — as
if by magic, thinned, and soon, at a very high altitude,
covered the sky, so it was all white. Darker clouds
beneath it were stirring into a dense, opaque turbu-
lence moving toward us fast, centrifugal swirls causing papers, leaves, sticks, light boxes and plastic bits,
etc., to go into a wild, hither and thither blow. Rain
appeared on the windshield. The sky became darker.
Tad flipped on his headlights, and stopped on the red,
at an intersection. The rain increased. The light turned
green, traffic began to move and the dark became lighter, and lighter as we drove, passing the park and turning on a broad avenue with two-way traffic while the
sky turned yellow. He pulled over to a curb and
parked.

"As that hole in the ozone widens," he mused, sitting back, both hands side by side on the bottom of
the steering wheel, as if talking to himself, "the

weather, including these rain clouds, gets more and more free blown—"

"No control."

"Yes. Look down at the end of the street."

I did, seeing a swirl of leaves and grit, dust, coming toward us.

"A little tornado!"

"That's it." Pause. "We don't have tornadoes here."

A cyclist passed us, and people on the sidewalk paused, to run to a tree and hold on, while the cyclist stopped, and gripped a no-parking post. Wind hit, car shuddered, and higher and higher, the sky swirled with trash. Metal waste cans on the corners went over, spun around. Awnings cracked like whips, windows and doors slammed, in a sound like a rising, dusty, husky whine, and whoosh, in an all-pervasive smell of damp and wet, the whole sky flung apart, everywhere—that great big sky, churning, swirling, spinning everything every which way. Small trees bent, some split, windows burst, shattered . . . the rain increased until it was a torrent, hitting the car at all angles, and hard. And soon over but it didn't pass like it used to. It went by ragged, capricious currents varying in their velocity, so at the end where the sky was a high thin layer of gray-white, with a dirty blue over the mountains— the sky and world were dirty. Grit, dust, lightweight trash, garbage everywhere, the air slow to become clean enough to breathe . . . it had been a vertical storm with circular violence, things swept upwards, cigarette packs, newspapers, small boxes, etc., plus dust, dirt, grit swirling up, up and around, to fall back

88

down . . . the windshield smeared with it, so too, we knew, the car.

"It comes so fast it can't be predicted."

"I know," I said. "Those people over there, look at them, soaked—"

"With dirty rain."

"This is all over the world."

"And it's gonna get worse."

He turned the ignition key, the windshield wipers still going, at length we could see what was ahead, and he pulled out into traffic. It was pretty ugly—this beginning, which is "gonna get worse." We drove to the restaurant, for a drop of something cool, before heading home—me to the motel where Madge was happy, swimming and getting some sun. I wondered how she survived the storm.

Before we went in, the blue neon sign in the window caught my eye.

Marie/Marcello on an angle in a bright blue script, bound by a pink neon heart, with a red arrow (Cupid's?) serving as a slash mark, except the arrow's tip extended beyond the top edge of the heart, and so too the feathers at the bottom.

"I see," I said. "That's Marcello."

"Right," Tad said. "Marie works the kitchen."

Being a little late today (the storm), the restaurant was quiet, a few couples finishing up lunch. The bar as well. Marcello washing glasses, and wiping down the bar while a group of four guys in suits, but wearing hard hats, just finished, were saying goodbye, leaving paper money for Marcello and telling him jokes while he — and they — laughed. Looking up he saw us, wiped his hands. Walked toward us, expressed pleasure.

"Well well," he said as we shook hands: "I wasn't sure if I'd see you again."

To Tad: "Hello. Always good to see you."

"Likewise." With a smile.

Marcello placed folded paper napkins on the bar before us, held up a rock glass, and a tumbler, raising his eyebrows, asked

"The same?"

We nodded.

"Good memory," I observed. "They don't make good bartenders like they used to."

"Because they no longer make good drinkers," he winked, with a smile, that beautiful smile Italian men have. "Personal company excepted," he added. Paused. "So, you win some and you lose some."

"Yes, and maybe better all round."

"I agree," he agreed: "You are a man of words who grasps my meaning."

Not sure how to respond to that, we smiled and didn't say anything. He drew Tad's dark beer, and began on mine.

A round woman with a square face emerged from the curtains, and waited until Marcello served us. Seeing her, he hurried toward her.

"Marie," Tad said.

Urgent dialogue.

Marcello signed, nodded, walked toward us.

90

"Big dinner tonight."

"Isn't that good?" I asked.

"Yeah, but it's a *lotta* work. We'll have the kids in to help, and . . . well, I ain't as young as I used to be, and this bending over, washing glasses, gets to me."

"You work the dinner meal, too?"

"Yeah," looking at me. "You know, I've thought about that, just doing lunch."

"That's it," I said. "Don't work too hard, you can't enjoy your job, and," with a look, "you don't want to get sick."

"Naw, *no!*" He exclaimed. "My brother's in the hospital, and —"

"There it is," Tad said. "Lunches only."

Marcello laughed.

"You guys are okay." And to Tad, pointing at me, "Is his poetry any good?"

"Oh yeah! *Real* good!"

"I knew it," with a chuckle. "And you must excuse me. I'm gonna take a break, go upstairs and lie down."

We shook hands, and he departed, so for a strange episode in transition, the bar was empty, and quiet, so Marcello's voice in the distance, was clear:

"Beginning Monday, honey, I'm gonna work just lunches, and knock off at five. Tell Anthony to come in."

He left out the "h" in the name, saying Antony, but even there, more like Antiny.

91

"That's wonderful!" Marie replied. "You'll be a lot more happy, and Antiny needs the money."

We left a good tip.

FRIDAY GOODBYE

My ride was late, nothing new in these jobs, where I depend on someone else for transportation. While I waited, out by the pool, where Madge swam laps. She swims like she sleeps: in long, slow strokes. She's not a short chopper. I warmed, watching her. Within myself I felt a peace, a philosophical balance, and harmony.

The weather, which had been cool and drizzle-no-breeze, warmed up. The sun came out, breezes riffled treetops and made little waves on the pool, as Madge said,

"See? I told you the sun would come out!"

Tad's car pulled into the parking lot.

"So you did," I smiled to Madge, bending down to kiss her, gazing down her cleft as she rose to me, made a naughty smile—she has a great body—I waved goodbye and walked away.

"I don't like this," she said through the fence.

"Nor do I," I replied, getting into the front seat. Tad waved as she made a sad face.

"What's that about? Or shouldn't I ask?"

"She wants me to stay."

"And you want to."

"You bet. She's more fun than anyone I know. We don't like goodbyes."

"Nice." Paused. "That's *real* nice."

"Thanks."

"You're welcome." Paused. Scratched his head. "What I meant was, also, it's nice to hear a man say that."

So, as we drove along through dunes and scrub brush into the city, the sky cleared, and I felt good. Poet that I am, I think I love to read next best. Philosophy is a favorite, for it forces me to think. Writing won't work unless we think, and remember our thoughts. Absorb them into our lives, thence into our work. Good for the creative soul. I may joke about Whitehead, but he's tops on intuition in *Process and Reality,* a book I read and re-read. This was my mood, as we drove: I was in part considering poetry as philosophy rather than direct expression, or metric structuring. So while we angled along city streets toward the prison, I pondered in reverie poetic aspects that put me in a very pleasant mood.

Yet as we approached the prison, turning into the parking lot, that familiar dread gripped my heart, my inner guts sank, and I was depressed. My loathing of it merged with having to go inside it — didn't want to go, but I had, of course, made a commitment . . . and with sighs at leaving my young driver-poet to drive away free, and me to go where I must, I made my way into the building ridding my mind of all preconceived notions and attitudes, so I could relate on an honest, objective level with my students. It has become a discipline, and I do it as . . . well, it's easy, in a strange way like leaving something, an aspect of my personality outside, in the parking lot—my ego, out there, while I go in. I don't miss it in the least, but on making contact later, after class, I feel good. But I have no thought of it inside. I don't, in truth, think. Or have fantasies. None! If I've said this before, I apologize, but it's true. I have almost no subjective involvement at all. Exceptions very rare. If I talk of my own work to illustrate a point . . . it's the most rare thing I do and in brief, for I'm in the room as a medium, more than a person. Which in its airy sublime leaves me vulnerable, so on slipping my photo ID under the sheet of tinted glass, and being told I had to have another form of ID, as well, I presented it without hesitation—always prepared—explaining I was here to teach. Mrs. Tracy would escort me to the classroom. But Mrs. Tracy wasn't here today, and that dim head behind the glass didn't know anything about it, having just come on duty.

"What should I do?" I enquired, leaning over, bending so as to project my voice under and up to whoever it was, there. "I have a class at one in classroom Number Four."

"Oh yeah?"

"Yeah," I said, as if it were always one prison, everywhere I went, and always the same man/woman blur, who only knew the rules, and nothing else.

A figure stood behind the outline to whom I was appealing, and I heard voices as three walking bodies, ID cards out, appeared behind me.

"Just a second," the voice behind the glass said.

"Just a second," I smiled to the people behind me.

"We know," they smiled in return.

"All too well," a man's voice sounded. My ear caught a tone of male authority. "I used to work here," it said.

Hearing nothing from within I turned to see who had spoken . . . my curiosity.

He was around six two, slender with small pot belly, in a double-breasted blue suit, light gray shirt, starched white collar and a tie the color and design not to match anything — all the rage today, this mismatch, in tomato-soup red triangles, splashes of pale blue, purple explosions mixed with jagged white and kelly green lines . . . His neck, face and large ears a pale, hardboiled egg color, with thin brown hair lines like long, flat grass, combed from left to right on top of his otherwise bald head. His eyes, behind rimless glasses, were small, and dark, with blonde lashes. Light brown eyebrows. Nose was short, blunt, broken, an indented mouth like a suture, a little too far down from his nose. Short, cleanshaven jaw. Looked at me with a patient, amused expression. Two women, one on each side of him, were with no expressions at all, they seemed, in truth to reflect the way he was. In my denim jacket, with its Teach Peace button above the left pocket. I smiled, in part to myself, as I turned, and bent over, to receive instructions from within, but as none was forthcoming I decided to step aside, and let them come forward, as they had all ID out, and were, it was clear, known to the administration, so I did. I stepped aside.

"I don't know what's going on," I explained, "but there's no reason to delay you, so—"

"You don't have to be defensive," he said.

"I'm not defensive," I said.

"But you are."

I looked at him and he looked at me. The women looked at us.

"I'm diplomatic," I said, stepping aside, as a voice within called my name, and I apologized to them, and stepped forward, bending over, and received instructions, my visitor's pass, with token coin, and key to the wall locker across the room. I walked away trying to fasten the clip of the pass on my jacket, as the man said,

"You're no diplomat," with a smile.

"Yes I am." I turned to him. "I teach in prisons. I'm a very good diplomat. I have to be!"

"So you say," he said.

"I do say!"

"George," said one of the women.

"If you don't like me," I said, taking a step toward him, "say it. Don't play games!"

"I didn't say I didn't like you." Red spots on his cheeks.

"No but you don't."

"How do you know?"

"The tone of your voice. The expression on your face."

"Aw *bull*shit!" Snarled.

"George!"

"You're being defensive." My eyes hard.

"I am not!" His wide.

"Yes you are!"

"How do you know! Prove it!"

"You're arrogant!"

"So are you!"

"Wrong. I'm angry. *You're* arrogant! Arrogance indicates insecurity —"

"Oh *yeah*?"

"*Yeah!* You're insecure therefore defensive."

A brown door opened in the wall to their right and the women turned to it, but he wanted to fight, yet the ladies were getting angry, prodding him. George, taking his arm —

"Come on!"

But he was angry, too, but they got him, and pushed him inside. Door closed.

I did a little dance, opened the wall locker, and after taking what I needed from my jacket, I folded and slid it in, closed the door, returned the key to the Shadow People, and proceeded to the door across the room as I had two days before, which after a harsh buzz, I pushed open. Went in the small short corridor, where a tall but thick woman guard waited, eyes avoiding me, in that, their proud prison tradition: door boomed shut, locked, behind me as the buzzer buzzed for the door in front, which she pushed open. We entered the corridor. *Boom.* Door. I explained which direction we were going, to number four classroom, down there on the left, and we began walking. She showed relief. At the door, which I opened, she was glad to be free of me, but I thanked her anyway for escorting me, and entered the classroom. Puzzled, as always, all prisons are one, so the guards at our sides so glad to get rid of us, for obvious reasons, no doubt: the responsibility of visitors (aliens) strangers in the home den . . . *go away! We don't want you!* They never say hello, or ask what I do.

My students all there, waiting.

"I'm sorry I'm late," I apologized, but they were quick to reassure, several voices saying everybody was late today.

"Any word from Sherry?" I asked Gina.

"Yes! She phoned Mrs. Tracy last night! She's okay!"

"Hey, that's great," I smiled, feeling blessed by her presence, opening my notebook and placing it on the same table I'd used Wednesday, with ballpoint pen. "We'll talk, later."

She nodded. The line of her throat under her kind expression, was a spiritual contrast to those fatigues. Her aura of peace, and empathy felt like a warm breeze in long green grass somewhere in the universe—here before me, I beheld her sweet, strong, willing life . . .

"Anybody bring work to read?"

Glancing at the young man who said he had, yes, he had written what I'd asked him to, I was delighted, even happy . . . but all too soon activities from unexpected (and I should have known better) sources came into collision, and caused such disruption the group forward motion—late in getting going—was delayed even further. And though I didn't know it to say it, aw yeah, I *knew* it, but who could quarrel with it?

My philosophical reverie with poetry, and the harmony it had created before and during the ride to the prison, jolted to an abrupt stop. In wanting to see poetry as philosophy I was avoiding the truth that this was my last class, so the good mood I was in was preferred over the hard fact that I would never see Gina, Sherry, Clipper, the sad woman and—all of them, again. So even in class, unwilling to admit it, reality entered with unusual bluntness. As I was unwilling to admit this group, young and old, African-American, Latino and white, men and women, all in one class—had never happened to me before. This original group inside a prison was revolutionary, and that I avoided the truth: today being the last of my involvement in it, as if snubbed, in a blue ribbon snafu, the prison itself came alive: a couple dozen guards got lost in the computer, and in the labyrinth of different billets and designations, nobody knew where those dummies were, so the calls rang throughout the prison, my classroom no exception, that harsh, grating electronic voice on the PA system — *Would Officer X contact Senior Officer Y for Duty Reassignment? Would Officer W contact Officer T for Duty Reassignment? Would Officer Z contact Control for Roster Revision? Would Senior Officer V contact Officers M, P and J for Duty Reassignment?* . . . etc., even with repeats! There was no talking in class while this went on.

The door opened, guards came barging in looking for guards! To witness the contempt they have for students, the classrooms, and you *know* education itself, right there! *On the spot,* the indifference they have for me — they hate me (being in their secret den), and the appearance they give, trying to fit the complex of their negative reactions into a mask of apologetic public relations is infuriating, and cause enough to rebel: *this* is the future! State uniformed men and women obeying orders absorb and transfer the racist, totalitarian corporate contempt, hatred, pretense and indifference, behind a mask, to excuse them for interrupting, all this, *all* of it! In *my last class* . . . who am I? They'll do it *in every class*!

I was beside myself.

"How can you stand it?" I asked, although I knew.

A guard had opened the door, come in, looked at nobody but around the room, searching, nasty-eyed:

"Excuse me," sneered. "Have you seen —"

"We have not," I said.

He looked at me.

"They're not here," I said. "Nobody. Just us."

"Sorry," but hating me for that, he left.

"How can you stand it?" I asked. Leaned against the wall, gazed up at the ceiling and closed my eyes.

"Stand what?" Clipper asked.

"The noise."

"What can we do?" a voice asked.

"It ain't up to *us* to stop it," laughed another, in general amusement. "Sure as shit nuthin' *we* can do!" Yet another.

"What we s'posed to do, tell the man to quiet down?"

Laughter.

I agreed.

"This is twenty-four hours, and where we come from, we don't even hear it."

"Truth is, we don't listen."

Well . . . yes, of course, I realized. Don't listen to it. So.

"You did your homework?" I joked—I was giddy—to the young man.

It wasn't a joke to him, but he was courteous.

Yes.

So he rose from his desk, and crossed to stand beside the monument to the paper industry that was even more today—what had once been Mrs. Tracy's desk. The black woman who had sat in a desk right there, was today at a table by the blackboard near the door. We'd smiled hi as I'd come in. Was this a religious experience, or test, was I being reminded once again, that the reality of existence was in the spirit of people? Not institutions? I felt like kneeling beside her, taking her hands in mine, and asking for the answers to it all. Would she forgive me? The poem she had read from her husband blaming Cupid for their wrongs, placed her in my heart, where Clipper, Gina, and Sherry were, too—the pale Garbo, and others. The impulse I had, to be near each of them, to solve what had gone wrong, to bring humanity to the foreground, saying, "Here. This is life! This is Clipper. He proves we are alive! Sherry, too. Gina, and this radiant black woman whose name I didn't know, with her deep, husky voice, and miracle laughter—this is the proof of humility, understanding and . . . a new focus for us! *This* is the answer! The proof! The vivid proof, of the utter beauty in being alive, to get them one by one, to tell us of themselves, to write it, so we can know, and put it together to see the world in a combined mind, and all-seeing eye, in these . . . this, collective spirit." *My last class!* What would I—But I

—didn't think of it. I—

didn't, but felt it, *couldn't* think it. No. Watched him open his notebook and, stand there, as no student would in any college or university, *want* to stand, face the class, and *want* to read aloud from work just written—*by hand,* not computer . . .

I folded my arms across my chest in a relaxed, standing position, my attention on him, hearing, seeing, nothing else.

Appearing casual, as he stammered just a bit in shyness, but gathered himself, and began to read . . .

He said (reading) thinking of street gangs in the way the media has presented them is too narrow, and what should be done in the world about children and violence was all wrong, that he agreed, gangs do replace family, yet saying in his eye there is no replacement for family, and while the other fellow had been right, where the point (emphasis) put was put on gang violence, it should be put on family violence because in his view, that came first, meaning we've got to rebuild the family before we can think of rebuilding violent kids, away from the gang violence they are drawn to for identity and meaning.

It wasn't a very smooth introduction to what he was going to say, for he paused here and there to go back, interrupting himself saying he'd never written these thoughts before — written to read before a group — which everyone understood, of course, but he meant, as an example of what he intended to say, how he had grown up, or not grown up in *his* family, and the problems he had had being the oldest, but not long after a sister was born, and after that another brother, his little brother, that his mother was pregnant with his little brother, but while part of growing up he wasn't at home, as much as he wanted to be, because his father was a drug dealer, and a user but in most part alcoholic — so he stayed away and I may be wrong, I only heard this once — but one night his uncle came over, or it was late, and he had been asleep, he was about five or six, and his mother, who was pregnant with his little brother came into his bedroom, followed by his father, no, he and his mom had been alone. She had come in, her left eye swollen shut, bleeding from her mouth, telling him she loved him, and he had begun to cry standing by the desk in front of the room, reading it, as his father came in demanding she return to the party they were having, and bring the boy with her, was having difficulty reading this, but he and his mother with his father went into the front room where a few men were drinking and smoking cigarettes

— his uncle was there — and I had the image of a small, rundown apartment, with worn furniture. TV set on, two or three guys passed out on drugs in chairs or on a sofa, as a couple of others were drunk or high, but everybody smoking cigarettes agreed to play a game, called chicken, had to find somebody who would go first. Who goes first? his uncle asked, and with his father's permission, even approval, one by one they put their cigarettes out on the boy's arm. His uncle went first. His mother screamed and lunged. His father hit her so hard she went down on the floor. Father went to her and kicked her in the stomach while she tried to protect herself as other adults took turns putting cigarettes out on the boy — he made not a sound, stopping to cry, wiping his eyes, the classroom in shock he continued reading what I can't remember, but soon after, or as soon after as things could be, he and his mother and sister moved away, and began life again in another city, yet his father turned up every so often, to beat her and depart . . . so they moved again . . . His little brother was born — had survived the kicking — was going to grade school, and doing well, but by then big brother was older and owned a gun because he had to. He never used it, kept it in the top drawer of his dresser, but one afternoon, coming home from school, on entering the house he saw the furniture had been knocked around, over-turned and there was blood on the floor. He went to his room to get his gun, but on entering, saw his mother sitting up on his bed, bleeding heavy from her nose, and his father, drunk, standing over her, the boy's gun in his hand. The boy went in, the father turned, mother lunged for the gun, the boy went for his father and tripped over a chair which saved his life, for he fell in such a way as his father turned to fire, and did, he shot him twice, in the leg and thigh, as his mother screamed . . .

He wept so hard he couldn't read.

The discussion was simple, brief, profound. And recognized a written work as well as an experience many of them had shared. Murmurs of recognition as he read, a couple of voices expressed "me too" and yet a couple more in a casual, offhand acknowledgement — "yeah" — at such violence, as if everyone were at home with it, hm? Say what? Problem? Problem? What problem? No need to discuss whether or not this written work was a success in reaching its audience. Its impact one of realistic documentation rather than minimal fantasy, or the pretend toughguy violence in detective fiction? This was not Columbia.

    Clipper, in a firm, deep growl:

"That took courage."

"To read or write?" I challenged.

He thought before he spoke.

"It took courage to write." Paused. "But it took greater courage to read."

    "Why?"

    "Because of us."

We got into a discussion of his first paragraph, awkward compared to what followed, not near that top quality and, as if a gong was struck, presto! The classroom filled with editors, all of whom agreed—me too, to hear it again. So the young man, who had stopped crying, and was sitting, on our request rose to read the introductory passage again, agreeing afterwards, that we were right! Wanna talk about fast learning! It should be revised to fit, to be more fitting with the work as a whole, yet . . . for of a sudden none of us was happy with that. The work was so strong, and at length we became critical of ourselves—I joined in, so in fresh group agreement by a show of hands—we let it be. Yes, it was therefore not a perfect work, but it was not intended—the author agreed—to be a polished, smooth piece of writing, no. It was what it was and many voices, mine among them, agreed to let it be. Great! All happy. Smiles, sense of achievement, balance and decision: letting what he wrote be the way he wrote it, in spite of the introductory awkwardness, for it was his way of getting going—beginning it. I remarked on the beginning of Mozart's Jupiter symphony, of Beethoven's Fifth—those famous first four notes being his way just as Mozart's. And many literary works as well. D. H. Lawrence's difficult beginning of *The Plumed Serpent*. The great beginnings of *The Turn of the Screw*, and Conrad's *Heart of Darkness*.

"Learn from it," I said. "This is how we learn from our writing, and on the next piece you write, think how you'll begin it, *before* you begin."

Feeling so good about that, I crossed the room and wrote on the blackboard,

Before you write, think how you'll begin.

Pleased even more to observe two or three persons copying it in their notebooks — the young man, too, and in a sudden anxious awareness, as I returned to the middle of the room, I changed direction, and walked around it, wiping my hands clean of chalk dust (on a bright purple cowboy hanky), I saw on the clock the class was over, and I thanked them for coming, I'd learned a lot, and wished them, each one, the best in their futures, as the door opened and a guard came in. I turned to him before he could speak:

"Nobody's in here except us," I said.

"No officer Fernandez?"

"No," I said.

Door closed. I laughed.

And that was that.

I shook hands with the young man from the violent family, who said one, I think, of the bullets was still in his leg . . . I encouraged him to keep a journal, and write about his life, giving it details, and lots of dialogue. I gave him my business card, and knowing he wouldn't I said keep in touch. He said he would. Nothing long and personal, just a card . . . I'd be sure to answer. I promised, and he promised, too, but I knew he wouldn't. How did I know? Ah yes, I was not in his world, while he much more, through an entrance to an art he was free in my world and my life, but I was not in his, so we said goodbye, I yet hoped as I always do, for in the way of being a man I loved the boy, handsome as he indeed was, with his light brown skin, and educated—but very tough—persona, as if a voice said, *Let him go. He knows you care. Let him go.* So. I . . . did, dying a little, I did, and left the room to say goodbye to Gina, who waited in the corridor, me feeling very near tears, not knowing what to say, or what to do, we hugged. It wasn't easy.

"I don't want to say goodbye."

She didn't say anything, looking down at me, from her mythical sky, I felt music . . . asked,

"How's Sherry?"

"She reported to her parole board yesterday morning."

"Things okay?"

"Yeah." The warmest yeah I ever heard. "She went by her boyfriend's and spent the night."

"Just as you thought."

"She's clean."

"Aw that's great."

Pause.

Gave her a card.

"Keep in touch, would you?"

She nodded. "Thanks."

"I'll want to know how Sherry's doing, and you know she'll never write."

She didn't say anything, looking at me.

"I'll answer," I said.

"Okay."

So.

That was it.

"Take care."

We shook hands.

There were no more words.

She walked away.

Didn't look back.

Her body had a beautiful swing, and halfway down the corridor, beyond the windows, as if to music, her hands moved out from her sides. Palms flat down, as if sliding along railings, fingers spread: in the swing of her step her hands moved back and forth, just out from her thighs, long legs, full, elegant body in those awful fatigues. At a corner she turned, was gone.

"Goodbye."

Clipper.

We walked along the corridor. Goodbye. Goodbye. Ah, but this was prison, not someone's nice hallway outside their bright, middle class apartment. There were no returns.

He said he was gong to get out soon, and I offered encouragement. I put a hand on his shoulder. He smiled.

"It's going to take a lot of work," I said. "It will be more difficult than anything you've done."

"I know," he said, in that devastated voice.

"You can do it, but it's gonna be, it's gotta be every day."

"I'm gonna go back to school."

"Good."

"I've done some studying."

"I know," I said. "But it's got to be disciplined."
He nodded.

We stopped at the door I'd leave through — which by chance opened outward by a guard who almost bumped into us. I grabbed, and held it.

I looked into the eyes in a face as dark as the far side of the moon as our hands met in a clasp. His was warm, smooth and strong.

"Take care," I said, despising myself for leaving him. But he . . .

"I will," he said. "You too."

Turned and walked away, just like that, making that space a separate, empty dimension as if by magic, the other body adrift, holding a door to another corridor open, while tall, shadowed figures behind tinted glass moved back and forth, in their electronic habitat. As far away as Clipper was, wherever he was, prison had made it impossible for him to stay, and see me leave so maybe I could turn, and wave to him just once more before going outside, or maybe I could say goodbye just once more, so maybe he could see how I hated it, and loved him, in this unjust, impossible impossibility, inhuman, uncaring, ignorant, cold and very, very nothing, this iron land of electronic shadows inside a tinted glass cube. So. Know what I did? I got out.

Out — I walked out of that house of walls and iron just like I always do, full of love in a blinding, crimson rage deep, deep down in my guts, that has words, these days. Words: *I'm gonna get you, prison system. I don't forget. I've gotten to know you: and my memory is long.*

But love and hate are dividers, oh yes, and I am mature and wise, I know I'm divided, that I love, and that I hate. So, what did I do? You know what I did?

I kept them separate, and mine, for I don't anymore mix them. I am no longer confused by them. My hatred, maybe like yours, is narrow but capable of expansion. It is intense, even blinding. It is inflexible, very hot, and although opposite to my love, the description is the same. Except in my love I have harmony, and the wonderful feel of tomorrow in the memories of yesterday, oh, if I could tell you of my life . . .

I used the key to get my denim jacket, put it on, slid it, and the Visitor's Pass, back in under the dark glass, and received my ID card, from those fingertips. I walked the length of the room with its enamelled-yellow cinderblock walls, and square of empty curved plastic chairs in the middle of the floor. I pushed open the front revolving door, and walked outside, the sun on my face. I walked along the sidewalk to the parking lot, crossing gravel to the car, where I opened the door, got in, closed it, fastened my safety belt, and smiled to my driver.

"That's a complicated face," said he.

"I'm sure."

"How'd it go?"

I stared out the windshield while he watched me. Ran a hand across my face, and turned to him.

"It kills me to leave."

He nodded: "Otherwise?"

"I can't begin to tell you."

112

He chuckled.

"I know what you mean."

We didn't even mention, not even a hint, *any* names.

Hey, walk outside free, and die a little, with them back there. Feel a sickness and sadness that's new, that you'll never get over. Say. Are you a little too self-involved? Too much you, you, you in your day-by-day routine? Well, teach poetry in prisons, and after class walk out free leaving your students back there. Get sick in a new way, with nothing you can do about it except realize your freedom is their gift: they let you go, so die, that's it. Selfish you. Die to discover a special gristle-tough non-ego gratitude as you witness them come alive in you, in your memory, your life and a sudden profound concern . . . Hey! Yeah, it's true: there *are* other people! They're vulnerable, creative and loving, and very angry, and they need you! So, give a hand here, join up in our Daredevil, Walls and Bars, Heartbreak Poetry Club . . .

Etc. Etc. Etc.

"I have an errand. Want to come along, or would you rather Marcello's?"

"There's a reason you ask."

"Yeah, it's an interesting drive."

"Let's go, we can fall by the bar after."

"Right."

So we headed east, away from the mountains towards the desert, always an experience, anywhere. Tad was knowledgeable about the city and its history, and as we angled along he gave me background on the different neighborhoods until we got to an avenue that headed, arrow-style, to the desert horizon, with one last section to go through, one more 19th century affluent neighborhood turned into a 21st century slum, and a bad one—mud paths, urine and human feces alongside the road. Shacks, amid old houses, crumbling masonry, shattered glass, cardboard and tin huts, and—the true expression of endemic poverty: poor people on the steps on government buildings (the post offices), and the same people by the side of the road casting long shadows, staring at the horizon, living like animals and multiplying, like green spores on blue meat.

Cars and trucks moved with us onto the desert, leaving that nightmare behind, toward an intersection that took my breath: T-shaped, in a plain, right out-middle-of-no *where,* we approached a huge sign, one of those double, left/right arrows, black on yellow, with nothing in sight pointing left, and right. But as if to bisect it, in the intersection, stood a tall, bright yellow stoplight. With the new style of colors, in big circles, glowing out.

"I bet you can see that at night, a hundred miles away."

"Planes look down on it."

We, with other motor traffic, slowed to a stop on the red.

114

"Which way are you going?" I asked.

"Left," he said.

"Go left," I said. "Always. Go left."

And on the green we did.

Toward a small-at-first but, getting larger fast, institutional compound with trees around it on black asphalt, with white zoning lines, yellow parking designations and blue lines for pedestrian traffic, to areas with benches and water fountains. Surrounded by a high chainlink fence topped with barbed wire.

"Well well," I quipped, as Tad laughed. "Home again. Classroom number 4, Officer, please."

We slowed before two columns of red brick supporting two 19th century wrought-iron gates, in the grand tradition, state asylum style.

A uniformed officer looked at Tad's papers, and waved us in. The asphalt was smooth and quiet, and he pulled into a slot not far from the entrance of this eight-storey, last century nuthouse. From where we were parked, however, low, modern buildings extended out in the rear property.

"The hospital."

"Why all the way out here?" I asked.

"The city used to *be* out here." Paused. "There were farms and orchards that fed the people, *all* the people, with a public streetcar system and its terminal right over there," pointing at empty desert. "Best in the nation," he said, "until G.M. tore it down in favor of diesel buses, and a new city hall opted to bring produce in from out of state, at less cost." Paused. "My granddad was a motorman, he loved his job. He knew everybody out here, on a first name basis." Paused. "In fact he was a poet. My work comes from his."

"Did you know him?"

"Oh yeah."

Tone of reverence.

"How important our grandparents are," I mused. "See a lot of that in prison writing."

"I *knew* you were gonna say that!"

"Because you've seen it, too."

"Yes!" Paused. "Be right back."

I nodded, as he got out, but turned, put his face in the window, and smiled.

"Thanks for coming along."

"You bet."

"Right back."

"I'll be here."

He strode, with a small, colorful bag in hand, toward the front entrance, as I sat there, observing the vista: patients, nurses, and visitors, here and there, standing, seated, walking, on black asphalt, under trees, on benches beside bushes, and flower beds . . .

The desert beyond.

Not quite sure what I was doing, or why or where I was going, I got out of the car, and crossed to double glass doors, with lettering, except as I got there, and looked in, it was a corridor, and as I opened a door and stepped inside I faced another set of glass doors, behind which another waiting area with chairs, low tables and potted palm trees.

Seated in a chair in an alcove, beside a window

116

on an angle behind a potted plant, was a woman I couldn't see, for her head was lowered, reading a magazine. She was slender to her waist, where she was overweight, even fat, with heavy, white thighs. She wore pink cutoffs, a blue tank top, and red sneakers, no socks. As if sensing me, she looked up—right at me, through the glass doors. But she wore glasses. I couldn't see her eyes, just tiny reflections of overhead square, neon tubing, as she looked at me . . . I wondered who she was.

"Hi," Tad said. "I'm back."

THE END

That Sunday Madge and me, with Tad and his wife Bea, drove up in their van to the mountains for a picnic. I shouldn't have said they were mountains, they were not the Rockies, but high hills. No snowcaps. Why did I say that? Well, there were lots of trees, and pollution as Tad pointed out, had played hell with the greenery down below . . . dry trunks, limbs, twigs . . .

But a nice day — sky criss-crossed with conflicting wind and cloud patterns, sun more dusty than bright, but it cleared as the day went on, and — as Tad described in his sardonic way causing Madge and me to exchange glances. Bea shared Tad's feelings, well, hell, who didn't? But there were other things to talk about, and Madge, a firm believer in conforming to local customs, and something of an actor, or stage personality yet very cool about it (only I notice), began to weary of it, in spite of herself, began talking slow, so the conversation, exception mine, spiraled down to a crawl, spaces between words, syllables had wings, tended to glide. I wondered what I was doing there, certain Madge was wondering, too. The motel where we were staying had a pool, and she was pissed off at having to come on the picnic. This was my job at the prison, and Tad and Bea were part of that, what was her obligation? So as her vowels began to get long, I knew she was getting weary of Tad's environmental cynicism, as he drove around rising curves, making critical comment, passing an occasional lookout view, until we arrived at the place he and Bea had mentioned. He pulled to a stop and we climbed out, taking our stuff across the dirt road to a clearing, with long, soft grass, tall pines and maples, some birch trees, too, beside all kinds of wildflowers, with a spectacular, unbroken view of the distant city and desert. We went to the edge, well, near the edge, and gazed out and down, identifying landmarks, close enough to see where we'd come from, far away enough to behold its splendor. The desert in particular, although even on Sunday, Tad and Bea remarked, there was a pall of gray blue over the land.

Spreading food and beverages on a blanket was fun . . . he'd brought some of his poems, and read them to us. I sipped a good local dark beer.

"Why don't you stay a couple more days?" Bea interrupted—I was complimenting Tad.

"Noooo," Madge drawled. "I've got to get back."

"Why?" Bea asked. "I thought you were freelance!" So Tad had told her.

"I am, but—"

"Come on," Bea pushed. Madge smiled.

"I want to go. We don't have to go, I want to."

"Why?"

"There are things I want to do."

"Like what—"

"Madge," Tad said.

120

Of a sudden Bea's face creased, I thought she was going to cry. Madge and I exchanged looks.

"My sister's coming for a visit, and—"

"I'm sorry," Bea said, not in the least sorry, getting an angry, impatient scowl . . . so sure she would be misunderstood, or ignored, no matter what she said.

"You like Madge, don't you?" I asked.

"Yes!" she exclaimed. "I do, and most often I don't but if— if you don't mind me saying you've got a way about you that . . . I like, and I *want* to tell you if you think that pool where you are is good, come with me to the one *I* go to!"

Madge laughed— we all did. Bea, too, as she opened her shoulder bag, took out an elongated, enamelled blue and silver compact which she opened, removed one of three joints, lit it with an eye-catching jade lighter, inhaled, passed it to Madge who did to it what was wanting, and passed it to Tad, likewise. The two ladies had leather lungs, it seemed, the insulated kind from the late Sixties. Madge, looking at me, holding smoke, gasped:

"Well?"

"Okay by me," I said, watching Tad inhale: the bright red dot at the end of the white weed got brighter and brighter with his hf-hhff-hhhfffff suction as his eyes got bigger and bigger, as he held smoke and looked out over the edge of the cliff, both hands raised, I handed him an open beer, he growled, like Clipper,

"*Thanks.*"

"Stick around," Bea inhaled— air. And quick,

exhaled as I had a toke, thinking it was gone, how wrong I was, had a toke, and it yes it was, it was *good,* watching a chicken hawk way, way up there, going in lazy circles. Madge said,

"Let's call the train station and go back Tuesday."

"Great!" I exhaled, and ate the roach.

We shared another joint, another beer, and unpacked the food like people do who are high on a nice day on the edge of a cliff, couple thousand feet up.

"Oh, *damn,*" Bea near hissed, to herself, "I *forgot!*"

She was tan, wearing a white tank top, pink shorts and blue yacht sneaks, had a crisp J Crew look, a solid three decades younger than me, lean from the waist up, but too heavy below, even fat, and too heavy in her thighs, bending forward, to dig in her bag, adjusting her glasses, she glanced at me, and smiled, and I had the feeling I'd seen her before. She wasn't wearing a bra, and her round youthful breasts were beautiful. Tad was busy watching Madge lay back, fold her hands under her head, gaze up at the sky: her mature, muscular body, white sleeveless, collarless shirt, cutoffs, green socks turned down, blue and white running sneaks. The tail of the shirt had slid up, as she'd folded her arms under her head, giving a view of her waist, lean tummy and belly button. Tad and I exchanged low, smiling glances, as Bea produced a letter half in and half out of an envelope, as she drank some beer, thirsty that day, no sooner finished Tad popped another. Her young long arms and slender fingers flew in haste to whip the letter out, and turning a bit away, with a darkened glance around, unfolded the note and began to read it to herself while we pretended not to watch. With a sudden cry she tore it in two, flung it away, yet a part fluttered onto the blanket before me, unnoticed by her, for she'd lowered her head, in tears, buried her face in her hands. Madge reacted, having seen — sat up, put an arm around her, which Bea liked, and allowed herself to be comforted.

"Stay another couple of days?" she sobbed.

"We will," Madge promised, looking at me.

I nodded.

"You bet," I said, looking at the half page on the blanket, text up . . .

"From her mom," Tad murmured. Shook his head, eyes to the sky, raising his index finger and thumb to his lips . . . this is what I read:

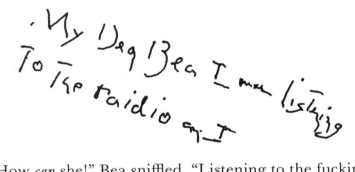

"How *can* she!" Bea sniffled. "Listening to the fucking *radio*!"

"Talk shows," Tad said.

"Yes, and they're *awful*!"

"Yep." Me.

"Yep." Madge.

So her mom remembered to write while listening to the radio (misspelled, note the interesting slip) . . . her handwriting told the story:

Individual letters split, separated from each other, the tailaway of her n's and r's, the whole text blurred, on a downslant, capitals mixed with lower case, the whole package indicating alcoholism, but more, too. The disturbing heart-shapes of the o's could mean a heart condition, all to depress her youthful daughter, no doubt sending her deeper down: overweight, drinking beer and smoking dope, desperate for the company of an older woman . . . but who knew the problems her mother had? And their origins? Bea took it as cruelty that her mom would have to be reminded by something mom heard on a radio talk show, to write, and be drunk as she wrote! Couldn't she perhaps wait until she had a moment of clarity, but! Maybe to mom it *was* that! Well, no wonder Bea carried the letter around, not wanting to read it — forgetting to, until in the company of Madge, and braced, with beer and smoke, which failed.

So here, I thought, we are. Three people who know what's going on, or should indeed know, who in this country can not? Fun Budweiser, a weekend with Michelob, Coors' Silver Bullet — these cheap machine beers and the teenage suicides, and accidents involved, continuing American self-destruction, ignorance, stress, depression and anxiety in a corporate consumer, money-crazy society? Felt a touch on my shoulder. I turned:

Madge.

Kissed her hand.

Soon the high was gone because the dope was not so good, but things had changed. Tad and I sat cross-legged, talking about his poetry, while the women, with some cool, went to pee in the woods.

We looked over the edge into the sky, and way out there he pointed, talking until I saw it, that long, long line of the prison avenue, from the abandoned miles of dirt, scrub brush, trash and skeletons of abandoned construction equipment . . . to the very green park, where the elder rich were dying feeling right at home. Across that avenue was the prison, inside which were Clipper, and Gina, and those other memorable people. Sherry had made it out, and was . . . somewhere out there, with all the city and desert and the sky beyond . . . I let hopes flow out toward her, am sure Tad did the same, although in a wistful way in this distance, as if they were sitting beside us. With a lost mother listening to a radio, and thinking of her daughter.

"Thinking what I am?" Tad asked, turning to look at me. We smiled, hearing the women returning, crashing through underbrush.

"I sure am," I said.

"My panties are wet," Madge said, as Bea laughed.

But Tad and I had turned, in our united thoughts, our heads had in one motion, gazed out at it, far away, but right there, across from the park.

And here we were.

Maybe that dope *wasn't* so bad!

"I'm starved," Bea said.

"Dope makes you hungry." Me.

Tad bit into a warm chicken wing, dripping with

tabasco sauce and blue cheese dressing, holding a stalk of celery in his other hand.

"Any lasting impressions?"

"The students. Always," I replied. "The students."

"Gina, Sherry, Clipper," he said to himself, ". . . wonder how Sherry's doing."

I was thinking of Sherry's drawings.

"You told me about Sherry's drawings," Madge remarked.

"Yes," I said. "That's what I was thinking about. How did you know? You don't have to answer that."

"Drawings," Tad asked.

"How did you know" Bea asked. Madge.

Madge gave Bea a wise smile, touching her shoulder with a fingertip: Bea smiled, that touch . . .

"We've been together so long I know when he has to go potty."

"I know when she has to, too."

Amusement.

Madge looked at me.

I looked at her.

"Drawings?" she asked.

I nodded, to Tad: "Sherry's an artist. She read a passage from her journal, where she's homeless, and—"

"Where she lives under a bridge in the park, by a drinking fountain?"

"Right. She stole a pack of spearmint gun and a potato."

"Ate the potato but saved the gum."

"That's it." I smiled. He smiled. We smiled. "In the dialogue and discussion that followed, among other

126

things she said Gina was her best friend, *and,* that *she* was an artist. Did I want to see some of her work?"

"I didn't know."

Exotic insects on warm breezes, with the sky-vista before us, made the talk as if an otherworld memory.

"Unh huh, well she, Sherry, ran back to her room, or cell, and returned with two samples . . . the first was pretty large, with a religious poem that Gina had written, in a script that Sherry painted in, like an ex-aggerated sized greeting card. But I knew what to say."

"Being an artist," Madge.

"He does his own book covers," Tad explained to Bea, who expressed pleasant surprise, saying she thought they were *real* nice.

I thanked her, I thought so, too: "And it wasn't that I was puzzled—"

"He's humble," Madge said. "Ever notice?"

Tad leaned forward in laughter. "I'll tell you," he said. "He's also very sensitive."

"Very sensitive person," Madge kind of cooed, rubbing my knee, "*very* sensitive."

"She strokes me," I confided.

"He loves it," she said. "Don't you?"

"Do you?" Bea.

"Yes," Madge declared. "Tell them!" Commanded.

"First she strokes me," I said, the proud husband, "before she licks me. I never have to tell her where!"

"Or how," Madge. "Soon we'll have no secrets."

"Don't blame me."

"You started it."

"I love to."

"We're not alone."

"Too true."

She lowered her eyes: Bea open-mouthed.

"Stop!" Bea cried: *"Please!"*

I applauded. "Yes!"

Madge: "Go on."

"It wasn't," I continued, "as if I was puzzled, or didn't know what to say to Sherry, I did, but I didn't want to be hi-hat, and overbearing, but she wanted response, so I responded."

"You said there were two." Tad.

"Yes. There were," as I stared out into the sky, remembering, even seeing them again . . . so.

I began:

"The first was large, but intricate, as if compelled that each detail be perfect. To copy a commercial pattern or illustration from a woman's magazine, *Lady's Home Journal*-type, where round, puppet children sit beside a round table covered with a flowery cloth, dish of fruit and vase of flowers in the middle . . . children reading poetry . . . both girls, the one on the left with the book in her hands, the one on the right eyes wide, listening. A cartoon cat curled on a round rug at the feet. Each girl in a gingham dress, very cute, very stylized, commercial, except that they were copied in prison, with rudimentary—at best—materials, not on an architect's desk, with an extension lamp, expensive colored pencils, sable brushes, Winsor Newton paints after several years education in fashion illustration—this was a prison distortion of what a convict artist considered beautiful, and meaningful: a slick smile and twinkling eyes became a forced grimace, and an anxious, even ironic, stare. Cheap colored pencils, gripped, and pressure applied to force the likeness through. Very intense labor, her head down, lips pursed, Sherry had done as best she could without erasing, so the careful blue and green checks in the gingham pattern of each girl's dress, following the folds round their thighs, and dip between their knees, tucks in the cuffs and shoulders, or ribbons round the tips of their pert little pigtails—stereotyped, with their freckles, turned up noses, that commercial artists do with such ease, saying: "This is how little girls dress in America!" which Sherry so envied—everything it represents—in the American Dream, of what she can never be because she never was." Sipped beer. "That illustration of impossible materials."

"What do you mean?" Bea asked.

"The slick magazines create appearances, it's how you look that counts, and artists copy that, creating an illusion of comfort, of being like everyone else, normal, and happy."

"What's the matter with that"

"Women in prison want to believe them," Madge said.

"But why not?"

"People who believe illusions don't face reality."

"I get it. Yes, of course."

"So," I continued, "if Sherry and Gina collaborated on a work, they created it because it made them happy to, a picture that was symbolic of what they never had, and never would have. Images of the unattainable. Men do drawings of sexy women they can never have. Prison is a place where illusion replaces reality. So, in Sherry's imitation of the slick magazine, greeting-card image of two girls, it's of a image she can never be."

"But how do you know?"

"Because commercial illusions are of types, not individuals, and Sherry was hungry to copy pretty girl-types, not real girls."

"You mean drawings of real girls."

"Right. "

"I see," Bea said. "Not what Sherry *is,* either."

"That's right, and that's the problem," thinking more than eating, with Madge making up for me, chomping away, "it's clear in the way they draw, as it is what they draw—and write—while they are in prison, that their lives are unformed. Talented, but unformed."

"Immature." Madge.

"Right. Because they draw like children do, early on, in elementary school, do an outline and fill it in, like Disney: a third and fourth grade art for the rest of her life. In her attempt to imitate the cute expressions, the superficial smiles, big blue eyes. But having no training in drawing or even in copying, it becomes ironic and surreal, because in not knowing how to draw, to create a happy human expression, they revert to what they *can* do, which is to only copy the image."

130

"That's primitive." Madge.

"Good." Ted.

"True," I agreed, "but it is the way things are."

"Boy, I sure am dumb." Bea.

Madge turned to her. "Sherry copied these lines, so the image became wooden. Stilted. Fixed."

"The hard outline that Disney used is the universal line used by artists in prison *and* on death row. It's prison art. And without using those words, that's what I told Sherry."

"You *did*?" Madge.

Ted and Bea laughed.

"What else could I do? I had learned in college the hard way, that the cartoon line I had used in high-school was too rigid, too controlled, too stylized, so I began to use my arm as I drew, no longer that finger-tip control. I did new, big work, pencil and ink . . . I told her her work was too tight, it had no imagination, there was no freedom in the line."

"What did she say?"

"You're not going to believe this. She was standing close to me, and Gina right beside her, as I held it out, like a big menu, so we could all see. A couple other students watched, too, yet Sherry was closest, against me, and Gina by her, Sherry almost panting she wanted response so bad, everything I said they nodded their heads, both, muttered, '*Yeah, that's right,*' looking at each other, agreeing, 'Okay, yeah! Good, anything more?' as I indicated the areas of rigidity, and lack of imagination. 'Draw bigger,' I said. 'This doesn't look like you at all,' I said to Sherry, 'you have more freedom in you, look at your writing, see? This is all closed in.' 'Ow! Yeah!' Gina cried. 'He's right!' Sherry beamed.

"What do you think of my poem?" Gina had asked.

Thank you Jesus, Savior, "I'm gonna tell you the truth," I said.

"Go ahead."

"I understand how you feel, but—"

"You don't like it."

"I'm not keen on organized religions, all of them. Look, in the name of Jesus, what was done to Spain, Mexico, Central America—*South* America, even here . . ."

"But we need it," she'd said.

"That's true." Sherry.

"I know you do, but that's belief, not expression. You're thanking God, not expressing your feelings."

"All right! All right!" Sherry. "What else?"

"Draw with your wrist, and arm," I gestured, "show more freedom in your work, quit copying this stylized, commercial shit, be an artist! Be creative! Be free!" Sherry gave Gina a punch in the arm, and yelled, "I *knew* it! I GODDAMNED *KNEW* IT!"

"Look at *this* one!" she'd said, showing me the other, smaller work on paper, and watching me look at it, with an arch smile, as I nodded.

"See?" she said to me. "*See?*"

"Yes," I said. "You can do it . . . don't . . . waste your talent."

"I'm goin' to art school in the fall!"

132

"What *was* the second one?" Madge.

"I can't *stand* it! *Tell* us!" Bea.

I ate the next to last wing, bite of celery, a couple of chips, had a slug of beer. Wiped my lips with a paper napkin.

"Right away I saw Gauguin, colors quite similar."

"Who's that?" Bea asked.

"French artist, very famous." Ted.

"Like Picasso?"

"Before."

"Much more exotic." Madge.

"Was Picasso exotic?"

"His Blue period," I said.

"What's that?" Bea.

"The period in his life where he painted only in blue."

"Is there such a thing? People, too?"

"Everything. People, still lifes, landscapes, the works, I don't know, all blue."

"How long did it last?"

"Two, three years," I shrugged.

"What did he do afterwards?"

"Cubism."

She lowered her head.

"I don't know what that is," she murmured. "I'm so stupid."

"Cubism is a period in art history," Madge said. "And quit being so hard on yourself. How can you know what you don't?"

"This is how you learn," I said. "How we *all* learn!"

"She hates herself," Tad growled.

133

"No I don't," she murmured.

"Do you want to learn about art history?" Madge asked her.

"I don't even know." She shrugged.

"What?" Madge asked.

"What what?" Bea.

"Do you know what you want to learn, or don't want to learn about art history?" Pause. "Why art history?"

"I don't know. I can't tell."

"Why?"

"I don't know. I like art."

"Are you interested in art history?"

"I don't know what I want."

"Do you want me to tell you?"

"Yes."

"Or do you want to find out yourself?"

"I want you to tell me."

Madge smiled, and looked at me.

"What's that look for?" Bea asked. "You looked at him."

"Why do you ask?" Madge.

"I want to know!"

"Why?"

"I said the wrong thing, didn't I?"

"Did you? You tell us." Madge.

"I did."

"What was it?"

Bea made a grimace pretending to laugh, and intended as a joke, or to be playful, hit Madge on the shoulder which jolted Madge sideways. Madge

134

therefore, hit Bea on the shoulder, which did the same. Except Bea's teeth clicked, eyes got big.

"I hate you," Bea said, rubbing her arm.

"What did you say?" Madge.

"You know."

"Tell us."

She pouted, ground her teeth, and fists white-knuckled. Head down. Monotone:

"You asked me if I wanted to learn about art history and I said I didn't know if I did and you asked if I wanted you to tell me I did or if I wanted to find out myself and I said I wanted you to tell me, which made you look at him, which made me realize I said the wrong thing I should have said I wanted to find out for myself."

"And?"

"I should want to find out myself but I don't know if I do." Head still down, talking in monotone, "I don't know what I want."

"Give yourself a break," Tad.

"There's so much to learn." Bea.

"It's important that you want to learn." Madge.

"You're smart," Bea said. "You know."

"Once I didn't." Pause. "What is it?"

"I dropped out of school," Bea confessed.

"School develops the disciplines we want."

Bea looked up, at Madge:

"Should I go back?"

"What do you think?"

"Yes," Bea answered. "Yes, I think I should."

"Good."

"But how do I know what I want?"

"Ask yourself."

"Just like that?"

"Yes. Before you go to sleep at night, ask yourself, hey you, that me what I am in there, what do I want?"

Bea laughed. "I like that."

Madge smiled.

"And that's it?" Bea.

"That's how it begins. It might take two or three tries, but you'll wake up with a dream, or a sign, that after you discover its meaning, you'll know."

"How will I discover it?"

"It will be such a surprise."

"Why will it be?"

"Because you won't at first know what it is but you'll feel it clear through, and be mystified. It will be very strange, very new to you."

"I don't understand."

"You shouldn't."

"But I'll—know?"

"The first clue will be your first understanding of what you gave yourself during the night. No matter what it is in the morning, as silly, as exaggerated, or simple, what that will mean will open the door to what you will want to do."

"You think I have all that in me?"

"I know you do."

"How?"

"You wouldn't fight it so hard, if you didn't."

"Your eyes are like the eyes of a cat."

136

Madge amused.

"She is a cat," I said. "You should see her tail."

"We're not alone."

"Alas."

Bea had taken a half pint of vodka from her bag, unscrewed the cap and tilted it to pour in her plastic cup of beer, but changed her mind. Screwed the cap back on, put bottle on the grass by the blanket.

"How," she asked Madge. "Do you know all that?"

"I live life. Every day."

"Well," Bea sighed, ran a hand across her lips, "I think I want to do that." Paused. "Where do I begin?"

"Right here."

I nodded.

Tad spellbound.

In an unexpected gesture, and I think unaware of herself, Bea was beautiful in that unformed way of youth, and innocence, therefore profound, a little like those other ladies. Her face radiant, as her eyes raised, in at first from a low distraction, to mystical recognition of sky under her slight, arced eyebrows. The sensitivity of her nose and lips was almost painful, she was so vulnerable: the pulse in her neck was distinct, as she gazed out. As if in a motion asleep she put her bag behind her, off the blanket on the grass, and reaching up, her torso moved in mythic uncoil as she undid her pony tail, her hair tumbled free to her shoulders. She turned, looked at Madge, and me, and in a different voice, with a more full or deeper tone murmured, we could read her lips, it was so clear, as she said she would begin at the beginning.

"That's *great*!" Tad.

But we knew the beginning was a relative thing, different to all who take the first step.

"Will you be my friend?" Bea, taking Madge's hand.

"Of course."

Looking at me.

I nodded.

"Could we go?" she asked Tad, who looked at us. We looked back. His decision.

"Sure," he said, rising, and with alacrity and our help, poof! They were gone. We assured Tad we could get back to town. In getting to her feet Bea had knocked over the cup of beer, but made no effort to set it right, or say anything, as if it never happened. We watched them go through the trees, carrying the picnic basket and their beach towels, yet no sooner had they left the clearing, Bea turned back and asked,

"*Will* you stay a couple more days?"

"We'll call the train station . . ."

"I can take you," Tad said. "Call the bookstore tomorrow, or drop by."

"Good," I said. "I will. We'll let you know . . ."

"Great."

Madge rose to her feet. Bea went to her. They embraced. Held tight.

"Thanks . . . so much."

"Keep in touch," Madge said.

"You mean—?"

"In the future. I'll see you tomorrow at your pool, but—"

"I will," the young woman nodded. "I promise."

"Until tomorrow." Madge.

They were gone. Silence. Engine started, went into gear, diminished, and we were alone. I mused—

"Weren't we cavalier, letting them go . . ."

Madge nodded. "That's a long walk." Paused. "But we can hitch."

"Only a mile or two to the highway, we'll get a ride."

And looking at each other smiled, recalling the many places we'd been, where we'd followed our thumbs down highways . . . "Remember that woman on Blue Island?" I asked.

"Who could forget? But I want to hear about Sherry's second painting!"

"Yes," I agreed, enthusiasm returning . . . "It was about this big," I gestured.

"That much smaller?"

I nodded. "The figure in the foreground, a woman, was so much a Gauguin I was stunned. Looking with those dark, expressionless eyes, right at you, both hands held out, palms up, holding a basket . . . that primitive, wooden style he had."

Madge nodded. "Yes. I can see it."

"In the background were three other women, and behind them trees and bushes, maybe a wall, or . . . facade of some kind, yet it was also like Frieda, the Mexican painter—"

"Kahlo."

"Yes. Frieda Kahlo, a mix with Gauguin, and—"

"What was in the basket?"

I held up a hand.

"I said to Sherry—"

"What were the colors?" Madge interrupted. "Were there any—"

"Yes. Pastels. Would you please? And I said, to Sherry, 'This is the way to do it,' indicating the open lines throughout the picture, except the delicate lines around the foreheads—bodies, head, hands, with no sense at all of filling in. It looked very modern, so much more open, and free, that the other seemed even more compulsive, controlled, it was hard to believe she had done both." I paused. Madge getting impatient. "Sherry standing very close, almost leaning against me, and Gina right beside her, both looking over my shoulder, Sherry touched the face of the woman in the foreground—

" 'That's me.'

"and moving it onto the baby—it was a baby in the basket, said,

" 'That's my baby.' "

"Was it naked?"

"No, even hard to see for the clothes."

"How did she react?"

"She was ecstatic. Strange."

"Strange?"

"The way neglected talent finds its ways—in the one a commercialized slick illustration, and the other a work of art."

140

"Didn't you say Gina wrote a poem — ?"

"Yes, for the inside of the big one. A religious poem."

"Oh yes," Madge nodded.

"Survival stuff."

"Ah," Madge said. "It's been a long day, and very rewarding, but the animals are getting restless." Lips parted with a sleepy look she came close, slid her hand along up my leg lighting me up, she cupped the fruit — getting bigger — and gave a gentle squeeze. "Mmmm," in an encouraging tone, like a sudden good taste, as of strawberries, "Ummm!" Came closer. A fast worker, me too — from the beginning, fucking before we knew each other's names — called me honey. "Hi, honey," unzipping my fly. "Look who's here." On the blanket, right there, *bam!* A straight dive. I pulled down her shorts, got panties off one leg, held her face in my hands kissing her very hot lips as she took out the stirrer, a husky, using both hands, slipped him in, and *allll* the way in, she gave a *big* strrretch, ran her hands along my sides as she moved back a little, held my face, big stirrer in, into the mustard, she moved this way and that he slipped back, and back almost out, her arms around me, back in around and, up, in, slow, messing up my hair, I had one hand around her ass, the other the back of her head she sucked air between her teeth, panting, sweating, like me, like me, in the grass on the edge of a cliff, under the sky, the sky.

Down the dirt road to the highway where we followed

our thumbs for not very long. A woman with two teenage sons in a pickup truck . . . We climbed up into the back, me being my age, not as easy, but Madge, in better shape, gave me a hand and we were in, and the truck was off.

Got out at the stop sign beside a bagel and something or other place beside a Greek restaurant named Aladdin's, I think, waved so long to our driver and her sons, all of whom smiled and waved back, heading east toward the desert.

So.

We went in Aladdin's, had some hot food, delicious — we were hungry after the mustard run, hot stuff I'll tell ya, plus the walk down to the highway . . . a figure approached our table hey it was Jay, Flattery, the guy who owned the bookstore. A tall, square-shouldered Irishman, a man with a way with words. I'd known him, though not well, for some twenty years. I rose, we shook hands.

"Join us?" I asked.

"Sure," he said, and sat down as a waitress appeared, greeting him by name,

"The usual?"

"Please," he said, and soon he had a bottle of dark ale, which he drank from the bottle, no glass. An at-ease fellow. Popular all over town. His wife had been in the movies . . . two talented daughters. Good people.

How's the book business?" I asked.

"Not bad," he smiled. "How'd it go? Tad was real happy, said you were terrific."

142

"He's a good kid," Madge said.

"Yes," Jay said. "What are your plans?"

"We thought we'd stay an extra couple of days," I said. "Bea says she knows a great pool near here . . ."

"Oh it is," he agreed, sipped beer. "Wait till you see it! Trees all around, and a little stand with the best hot dogs, *and*— best root beer this side of Kansas City!"

We beamed.

"How's the family?" Madge.

"Wonderful. I'm here to pick up supper. We're going to a concert—" his youngest daughter was performing. Did we want to come?

Sure! But we were wrecks, sweaty, and—

"No no, it's outside, in the park."

"We'd love to!"

So we did. On the way with them, in his van Madge shifted this way and that up against me, and beside me (whispering) mustard was running down her leg.

"Want a hanky?"

"Aw no," she said, giving me a lick behind my ear, "I can wait . . ."

So it was Chopin under an early evening sky. Beautiful.

The next day we went for a swim in that pool, had a couple of dogs and some root beer. Bea was serious, and thoughtful. Talked with Madge, I don't know what was said, but a couple of days later, we said so long and took the train home, or rather, stopped by the bookstore, so Tad could give us a ride, but he wasn't there, nor was Jay. Instead there was a note, on bookstore stationery, that said Bea was going home. To take care of her mother. Said Madge would understand. Tad was taking Bea to the airport, he'd be in touch, as would Bea . . . thanks for everything.

But they didn't keep their word. We never heard from them again. Tad kept working at the bookstore, and not long after we left, met another young lady. We never heard from Bea. But, she'd begun at the beginning, we'd talked about, that day in the sky. her going home to be with her mom made us disappear. But Madge knew that, so did I. That's the way these things are. Freedom is just another word for a different kind of prison. There's a joint with walls and bars for every one of us, in every town, city, state . . . Bea got out of hers leaving a half pint of vodka, opened but untouched, and a styrofoam cup of beer, and went home to get her mom free, too. And in that effort we didn't count. Why should we? Something she had to do. Madge had done it. So had I. Bea knew.

Well I should have known, with my bad memory for recent events, typical of my getting old . . . we didn't hear from Tad which didn't surprise me, but I was disappointed because I'd liked him a lot. Yet he was a young poet in his own town in his own life, and while I'd been there it had worked, but after I left, I was gone. He didn't follow anybody.

Bea *did* write, but it wasn't for several months. Madge said, if I get can get this right, that we got a letter thanking us meaning Madge, but because Bea was polite she mentioned me, too. Said she was okay . . . no, I should say that, she said . . . wait. First things first. Her letter was handwritten, on blue lined notebook paper with a black ballpoint pen, like I see in prison writing, except Bea's had more freedom, the tails of her e's, n's, l's, t's, etc., had a healthy upward curl, and the dots above the i's and t-crossings were centered, although a little high, which was good, as her capital letter I, and lower case g's, f's, and y's ballooned out below lines, suggesting sexual hungers, but why not?

She said she had gone home, to discover her mother was hospitalized, so Bea had taken care of her, gotten her home again, and done what she could until her mom died. But a *lot* happier, than if Bea had not been there. They'd become close, had long talks about her mom's life, and also, her dad, what had happened to him, and his side of the family. Bea had begun therapy while there, and began keeping a journal. While beginning to teach a physical therapy group (hoping to go higher in education), she had met a young intern and would she guessed marry him although he seemed too immature, but she liked him quite a bit, and . . . to get her head straight took a vacation, before she returned . . . thanked Madge again, and me. Remembered that day in the sky . . . it had changed her life. Please keep in touch, she would, too.

Gave home address and phone in Minneapolis, but her letter was postmarked Fortuna, Costa Rica.

Madge went into a sentimental fit, knowing Bea was in Fortuna, by the lake, near that great, great Volcano, the Volcano at Arenal.

Memory and dream went walking along up the flank of that towering Volcano . . . majestic, archaic, primordial and profound onto a cliff overlooking the sky and the plains with Tad, Bea, and Madge, beer and Buffalo chickenwings, with the long highway in the distance, the park for the dying rich and across the avenue that prison, where I had said goodbye to Clipper, we'd shaken hands and I'd tried to say important things to help him, as I'd put my hand on his shoulder. Oh that implacable face.

And Gina, the mysterious, mythic Venus, and the woman named — I remember! Carla, whose husband, from a federal prison had written her a love poem of Cupid. He was in truth, Cupid himself. Mrs. Tracy, the super supporter of prison education: She Who Made Things Work. And Sherry, looking at me, standing so close as I held her art, my left arm almost around her — and Gina, that close to her, as we three looked at it, at that other, most enduring myth of all, an even deeper orange in the orange: the Alpha of Mother: The Woman Holding the Basket. Madge had asked because Madge was intuitive: "What was in the basket?" Sherry's baby, so Sherry, the writer, the artist, was mother. "That's me," she had said, and pointing to the baby: "That's my baby." The three women in the background, kin to Gauguin, and Frieda Kahlo, three women against what I remember as a wall, why not say the whole wall of existence, with mother holding her baby in swaddling clothes in a basket, for us to see: an image, a work of art, a creation by a young woman in an American prison, to be remembered by a man who saw her just once, just once, before she went free.

I forgot to say that Tad and I had gone back to Marcello's but he wasn't there. They'd had a busy lunch, and his kids—in their twenties—were helping out. We got served by the good looking, dark-haired daughter, on the plump side, like her dad. She and her brother were joking about him, and the horses.

"Where is he?" I joked. "At the tracks?"

Well, *that* was *a laugh,* as she placed our drinks before us, paper napkins an afterthought . . .

"Aw no. That's tomorrow. He took my little brother Joey to the doctor."

"Joey couldn't go?" I asked.

"Yeah! He could'a', but Daddy wanted to go, you know."

"Sure."

"He knows," Tad said.

"Get that cast taken off."

We nodded.

"On long?" Me.

"Three months."

We exclaimed, in unison: "Wow."

"Excuse me," she gestured. "I've got to—"

"Of course. Don't let us—" Me.

"What I like about you," Tad joked, as she began

washing glasses, "after two visits you become a member of the family."

I shook hands with him . . .
"Sure you won't come in for a swim?"
"No," he laughed. "Thanks."
"Okay. See you Sunday."
"Sunday it is."

He drove away.

I crossed to the pool, just outside our motel room. Madge lay on a chaise reading one of those magazines she never reads, left by someone else.
I went inside, changed into swim trunks. Came out. Joined her.
"Hi," she said. "How'd it go?"
"Wonderful. How're you?"
"I don't have my period."
So.
There we were, beside the pool which reflected the sky, and the mountains — hills, low on the horizon.

That night we watched reruns, back to back, of the only two shows we watch on network television: *The Simpsons,* and *Roseanne.* At one point, I can't remember where, we agreed the effect, in memory, of their combined dialogue, reminded us of ours.
"Yours," Madge said.

She seemed to be in a mood, so I didn't tell her about

148

the picnic Tad had planned, pretty sure she wouldn't like it. It had been, after all, my job. She hadn't met anyone, at the prison or the bookstore. What was in it for her? Another obligation? No, she wouldn't like it.

I stretched out beside her as she slept, and watched a moon rise over the pool, the parking lot and the hills, into a bright, star-filled sky.

May 28–August 18, 1993
New York

Hands Like Titian's Venus

"He's a fascist!"

"How do you know?"

"I used to go with his ex-wife, and—"

"You believe ex-wives?"

"I believe this one!"

"Just kidding. What did she say?"

"That he was a fascist. He defended Metzger on separatism and read the many histories of Nazi Germany. The Speer book in particular."

"But of course! Look at his work, creamy smooth surfaces, same roundness . . . that repressed presentation of massive facades—pure totalitarian."

It was true. People who knew him would agree, but not those that didn't, because he didn't talk about books, or ideology, with anyone—he didn't talk much at all, just didn't like it, so you got to know him by his work, his actions, and, well, his silence. He could hit a woman, maybe a man, but a woman, yes, and the ones who knew him, knew that. Though he was a small man, not short, but small and round in his way. With thin black hair, a receding hairline—his head as round as a baseball his face in the center: almost no chin, small, pink ears, tiny lobes, pug nose broken from a childhood fall. Black eyebrows, like Duke Ellington's mustache, slanting up just a little at center, gave his deep, protruding English blue eyes, with opaque pink lids, the shocking look of real eyes in statues. It fit. His work in acrylic — minimal, of course — painted geometric cubes with rounded corners, edges, in pale grays and the most pale pinks, on off-white ground: images seemed to float, effect of looking at nothing that looked back at you. And *big,* boy the work was *big,* a whole roll almost for one picture!

But he had a big studio, a few friends. Men. The kind that deferred to him. Because he was silent he was seen as wise, thoughtful, and sly but in truth he didn't know what to say, because he was *not* a thoughtful man, he was hot tempered with a short fuse, those dark blue marbles in his head got big, and he flushed crimson, something to see.

Everything had its place, in his studio, and of course at home, with her, which she knew. So he was neat, even his paint clothes were clean, not a problem to her, so to all appearances, they lived like everybody else did, he tended to sit up in his head and be only for him because he was an artist, but she didn't mind. There wasn't a lot to be said. It all seemed simple.

Not so.

They were easy to look at, but difficult to read.

He had a good reputation without being famous. His work sold and in fact he was something of an art writer, like Donald Judd (whom enemies dubbed John Dudd), on art, even an academic, well, he fit. He had

154

his degree and he taught, this smallish, dark blue, all white fellow: older than she, but younger in his moody, childish compulsion on neatness, yes yes yes intelligent, well-educated all that good background stuff. But he nagged—he'd been spoiled by his mother, and was combative, in that tight, academic habitat where the males hiss, show their teeth, and spit, if things didn't go their way. Say after a meal, and she hadn't cleaned up—even the mess she'd made cooking. He'd not say anything, but scowl, glare at a serving spoon left on the table.

"What's the matter?" she'd ask.

His face turned red. He bared his teeth and hissed, pointed, spat:

"That!"

Which she hastened to pick up, and put in the dishpan to soak, making sure to wipe any spot, left on the table.

He preferred to let her do the nine-to-five, rather than bother. His one day a week at school . . . so she paid the rent.

She was a serious, earnest, loving younger woman. Smart, fun in company. Gregarious, outgoing. His opposite.

But for a reason he perhaps resented, the friends she had she couldn't speak to in a deep, confidential way, as if forbidden, she wouldn't speak, and became locked within, while his friends, who went a ways back, were in no big way a surprise, being a lot like him, deferring to him. Stayed up all night, drinking white wine and, as their apartment was small, she—being sociable — and unable to sleep, joined in, to listen. Got to work late the next day feeling rotten, and angry, but of course didn't want to upset him. One night she was late making supper, he smashed a serving platter with a hammer, another night he slapped her. She hadn't flushed the toilet. If she prepared meals he didn't like, he wouldn't eat them. She also did the shopping. He came home from his studio and wouldn't go out. Stayed in and watched tv. So after she came home from work and from shopping there he was, watching CNN or old movies. But, she loved him, he was at least there, and if this was the way he was, she could live with it. It could be worse. They had fun together, doing what he wanted to do, go to a neighborhood bar, and watch football. Last August he spent a month in Key West with his brother, on bro's boat, and she missed him. Sure. She phoned every night. Dutiful, and loving, but, who knew? He'd had several affairs before, been married, there were women who liked him. He didn't talk about it . . . if things went his way, the world was okay, and he agreeable, amusing, not bad company. Meaning if things did not go his way, he'd be the opposite, which was true, but if the world to him were harmonious, it didn't include her except as she responded to it and to him. She, smart enough to not want to upset him and, in truth, as he was older, she allowed he was wiser. Which was the key to his deception.

In social situations where he didn't know what to do or what to say, he put on a mask of wisdom, a stoic demeanor which impressed, even thrilled her.

156

And made it, no, it — it created an illusion about his past, as if it helped his mystery because we think of the past as mysterious, even if there is none. There was nothing mysterious about him, except the image he created for others who believed it. And she did, so, in character for her to reason, she saw him as she knew him, not as she did not. He had no curiosity about other women, and as she seemed to please him, why bother? Relationships were not easy. Her friends were impressed — or so they appeared. Nobody liked that bastard. But it was true, he didn't talk about his past, and the women — or his wife — but he let her know, at home, oh yes, it was none of her business, so with the mystery he added his nastiness, yet she saw him not as nasty, but aloof, more wise . . . which he took full advantage of. Like quiet people who in some sort of magic, having done almost nothing in their lives, being very near no-people, with almost nothing to show for it, except collections of "things" in bronze, gold, and precious stones, maybe even stamps or coins — with him his art, these repressed, quiet/violent types are often fine actors, in the part — for it is the same part they played, these men and women — putting on that mask of wisdom, above it all, with a sleepy-eyed smile: *I've been around, you know. I wasn't born yesterday.* Everyone laughs.

Even sophisticated people, who enjoy the obvious, but for a different reason: the deception was acted by people on stage, not out in the world, living among people, and the dynamics of existence, no. To say *I wasn't born yesterday* was not a strong point in his character, but a defense against it.

This is why he was jealous of her.

Being young she wanted to live, out in that big, tough world, but didn't know how. She saw him as part of that world. And preferred her illusion.

Which he had to maintain. Because, in truth, even to him, as he saw himself, he more or less just "grew up," meaning he couldn't figure her out. Those long silences. Was it him? Or the way she was, and not him, so there was an unanswered question: how had he affected her? To the depth of his wish for power, or as a young woman in an affair, awed by him?

Well.

At her job she made friends with an older woman, and she began talking, at first, about her enthusiasm in music. The woman's father had played trombone in several big bands in the late 1930s and the 1940s, so had grown up hearing all those records. The younger woman had had a crush on a guy in high-school who played tenor saxophone, even as a teenager, with groups, had real talent, dreamed of starting a band, but died in a car crash. Her older brother loved that music, too, and once at lunch, both women sang together, that awful song, Woody Herman, Frances Wayne on vocal: both women hunched over the small table, eye to eye, one as if playing a trombone the other a tenor sax . . .

"It seems that happiness, is just a thing called Joe . . ."

Both closed their eyes imitating the screaming trumpet section following, sitting back laughing . . . misty . . .

"The words were so dreadful, but the music so great."

"Yes," the older woman agreed. "The one thing wrong with Woody Herman's band was Woody Herman."

So.

It wasn't long before the younger woman opened up about her boyfriend, the artist.

By chance that woman met him. He stopped by after work one day, to take her to see a movie he wanted to see, and she introduced him:

"Lucia, this is my boyfriend—" Paused. "He's an artist."

"Oh, pleased to meet you."

She saw, right away, that he was the dominant figure of the two. If you saw them on the sidewalk, walking toward you, it was him, with her in his shadow, and he liked that, he *liked that*. But he did *not* like her, right away. This woman. His eyes darkened, and he bared his teeth in a smile.

"Thank you," he said.

Feeling a *sssss* coming on.

The older woman laughed.

And some while afterwards, the older woman mentioned, with diplomacy, of course, that her boyfriend, that day they met, had not liked *her*. Right away, she said, she saw that, and the young woman, smarter than she knew, agreed, yes, he's jealous. Quite so, the other agreed, because baby would be, and, as a grown up baby, suspicious.

"His mother—"

"I know," the older woman interrupted. And later, at home, watching a FRONTLINE documentary, on the U.S. sales of arms to Iraq, before the Gulf War, this small, neo-fascist bluish white man, round around the edges, with his vicious — even cruel, academic know-it-all glare, in a relationship with his near-victim.

Who had been brought up in one of those large, all male pro-labor families: the little sister in a pack of big brothers: football, baseball, hockey fiends, among them her favorite, oldest brother who, after their mother died, and Dad just fell apart, he'd made a point to care for her. He saw her through high school, helped her with homework, through the tough teenage years no mom no dad, well she loved him beyond words, and after he came home disabled from Desert Storm, she saw her chance to repay him, which she did with such verve and dedication he saw her spending the rest of her life at it, so, listening to the big band records they loved so much, he decided it was wrong for her to stay home and told her to leave. Go to college, get a degree, meet a guy, and get going in her future. So she did, because he'd told her to, but, it wasn't easy.

For taking care of him had become not a mere habit, but an absolute state of mind: she avoided her future, which he saw, and they talked about it, he said she was avoiding becoming a woman, that she was too quiet, she needed friends, and to open up, and in a way she died, because she didn't want to just *care* for him, and hang around at home in his life, she wanted

160

to *merge* with him, wanted to be in his body, and run with the blood, like the drum, brass and wind sections, in the high flying trumpet solos, and be the beat of his heart.

What was his name? Hey.
Joe. Happy?
What do you mean?
Why did you ask that?
Why did you answer?
I wanted to see what you'd say.
Did you get what you wanted?
Yes. In Part.
In part? What else was there?
Nothing.

"You see it right away."
"Where?"
"In its obvious ways."
"Where—"
"In front of your nose. It changes."
"I see! What you see is what it is."
"Yes, but changed."
"Which means?"
"Very little *if* it's compelling. This is delicious."
"Hits the spot!"
"Mmmm . . . I didn't know I was so hungry."

In a neighborhood, fast food joint: an East Indian restaurant. Two people. A man and woman in their mid-late forties, seated on plastic chairs, facing each other over a small, formica table, enjoying curried chicken legs on saffron rice, with boiled cabbage and condiments, drinking cold, Eagle beer. Afternoon sun shining through the windows, as people walked along the sidewalks outside, all bundled up in the January freeze. Cars and trucks crawled and beeped and honked like big toys, while bike messengers zig-zagged through: frosty dragonflies.

Indian teenagers crowded around an older woman at the cash register up front, their young voices, to her maternal amusement, sharp in laughter, in the warm, steamy, spicy air.

The man and woman at a table in a corner by the window. She wiped her lips on a paper napkin, and said,

"I met him one day after work. He had stopped by to meet her, on their way to a movie . . . he was jealous, right away I saw it. His eyes got dark, like a cat's." Pause. "You know."

"Thank you. I do. But he's not that old, is he?"

"Older than she by at least a decade, but to us young, the quiet type. Sullen. Hostile."

"All too often true."

"But where he was obvious, she was not, yet he appears to define them! In truth it's—"

"How can she stand him?"

"I asked that myself! How *can* she put up with it? Day after day! Coming home from work—" gesturing

162

with her fork—"*after* shopping to prepare a meal he might not eat!" She sipped the good, cold beer, averted her face to look out the window.

He watched her: *she's beautiful. No, she's handsome. Striking!*

"There he is!"

"Him?"

"Yes! Over there, on the corner, waiting for the light to change, in the yellow scarf, that fascist!"

"Ah!"

"Yes! Look at that book under his arm! See? *Totalitarian Architecture!*"

The white, winter sky reflected in her brown eyes and, he thought, as he watched her stern focus on the fellow with the yellow scarf, walking across the street, with a book under his arm, that she was lost to him. She spoke:

"Why are you looking at me?"

"I'm not sure . . ."

"What is it you see?"

"I find you very attractive."

"Why?"

"The way you are," he lied, and she asked, anew: "Why?"

"I'm not sure," he fibbed. "You're very good looking," feeling better for the truth, in awe of her questioning him. "But I don't know you."

"Yes," she agreed. "Nor I you."

"Do you regret my asking you here?"

"No!" she exclaimed, with a smile. "Thank you!"

"You're welcome. My pleasure, in fact let's come again."

"Yes . . . I might like that."

"Interesting."

"How so?" She blinked because he had caught her off guard. She hadn't thought he would say that.

So, her question stopped him. He wasn't smart enough to know where to stop being honest, but he wanted to be, and wasn't sure what to say.

"I want to be honest."

"Yes, we must be, always," she agreed, her gray eyes, like targets, on the inside of his head. She'd known a lot of people in many different locations under a variety of circumstances, so his feeling of having to say something because she made it so, was correct. The ball was in his court because she put it there.

"I like you," he said.

"You don't know me," she repeated, with a very near coy expression, pretty sure he was lying. Maybe he's a liar.

"That may be true, but I—I like you anyway."

"So far," she smiled.

"Yes," he chuckled. "Thank you."

"You're welcome, and, for what it's worth, I like you, too."

"So far," he smiled, but he shouldn't have said it, for they were her words, which she had given him, meaning he had little imagination, was poor in response.

She didn't say anything, enjoying her lunch.

164

He didn't know what to say.

"I apologize," he almost stammered. "These are high stress days. We are all preoccupied with ourselves, involved in our own thoughts, needs, and passions. You pursue yours, and I mine, you your way, I in mine."

"That's true," sipping Eagle beer. "But we are not *all* self-preoccupied, although it may appear so. I was involved with Unicef, in Central America for several years. One of my jobs at your—or *the*—company where we work, is learning advanced computer technology."

"Why?"

"Corporations from all over the world are destroying natural habitats so fast we can't keep up."

"Why should you keep up?"

"So we can stop them."

"Oh, I see." Paused. "You must think I'm very—" at a loss for a word, "stupid."

"I wasn't thinking of you at all."

"What were you thinking of?"

"The Dole corporation killing native-slaves and poisoning the Caribbean."

"You're only here, in part, with me."

She adopted a kind expression. "Yes."

"You're not pretending."

"No. I don't do that." Paused. "I do other things, but not that. I'm not that clever."

"It isn't a big thing."

"Not unless it becomes so." Paused. Lowering her gaze to her plate, he saw she was between decisions, as women can be, so she raised her eyes to meet his: "But it doesn't have to be."

"You're too smart for me."

"Are you sure?" she asked, expression worried. Anxious.

He didn't know what to say. "No," he began, "but I feel—"

"I have intense commitments, but—"

"I—I don't want anything to—come between us."

"Nor I."

So both were relieved, somewhat, and became involved in their food, finishing all too soon, it seemed, their beer. A waiter, a boy, floated over, and smiled down at them, seeing the man ask the woman:

"Okay for another?"

"No," she said. "I have to be clear-minded."

"Split one?"

"Yes!"

"Fine," and to the waiter: "One Eagle. Cold, please." As the boy looked at them with the keen, exotic eyes of a foreign child, who turned on his heel in an elegant way, and crossed the floor, hand raised.

"One Eagle beer, cold," to his brother behind the counter, and soon the couple at the table shared that beer, the man—not the boy—pouring it into the two clean glasses given them.

"Thank you," she nodded. Raising glasses, touching rims. Drinking. Mmmm, good. "But why did you say that? You made me self-conscious."

"Say what, oh yes, well, you *are* smart!"

"In tracking multi-national corporate moves and decisions, you can't blink, they're so sly, so I'm good on concentration. Sustained concentration, but I don't think I'm smarter than—you, or anyone. No. I'm not."

He was impressed.

"May I tell you the truth?" he asked.

"Have you not been?"

"What is it you want?"

"The truth at all cost." Her face a mask, for he shouldn't have asked. The ball had not left his court. He was hitting air.

"Where are you?" he asked.

"Right here." Paused. "Why do you ask?"

Two balls in his court. His lips parted and he blinked. She was looking at him.

"I thought I saw you disappear."

"And how did you feel?"

"Unsure."

"Of who?"

"You are—"

"No, I'm not. It's easy. Tell me," she murmured, her face soft, and almost moving forward.

"Unsure of—" he licked his lip. She murmured:

"Tell me."

"Myself."

"Yes."

"What else—"

"How could you have been unsure of me? You don't know me." Her lips parted, he saw the rim of the glass tilt, and the liquid go in her mouth.

She swallowed.

"What I mean is you can be unsure of yourself in any way you want," with a warm smile, "and I'll do the same, but don't assume any uncertainty. Not yet."

He nodded, a little lost. "Okay, but why?"

"We'll regret it."

"Because we'd be disappointed?"

"Do you have to ask?"

"No. We would be. I would. You're right."

His body warmed in a heavy, sudden yearning for her, and she withdrew, a little.

"I don't like people who try to figure me out, but I like you — so far, although we don't know each other. I feel in a way, I'm getting to know you."

"How should I respond? And I know you, too?"

"Why ask?" she taunted.

"Why not?" he asked, angry, which she saw.

"Ask yourself," she said, tilting her head up, and looking down her nose at him.

"Stop playing with me."

"You're getting angry."

"Wouldn't you?"

"Yes." Paused. "I'm sorry."

"You make me a plaything. If we don't know each other here today, how will it be — later?"

"That's true." Paused. "I am sorry."

He placed the cheap silverware on his empty plate as if both cost thousands. Wiped his lips with the paper napkin, like silk.

"Let's be spontaneous with each other," he said. "Don't make me defensive. I don't want to get

168

angry at you because I don't want to regret it."

An irresistible fire swept through her, causing her to want to *explode*: *What would you do if you were in love and were angry? Would you be more real?* Wanting him to be both, seeing him hungry. She pointed her chin at him.

"Do you lie?"

"Yes."

"Why?"

"Because I'm a liar. You?"

"Yes, and I can be . . . evasive."

"So you *did* disappear."

"Maybe you're right," she said, raising a finger, "but maybe you're not."

"I know I'm right."

"How do you know?"

"Women go away from men."

"That depends on the man."

"Not if he knows anything about women."

The ball was in her court, and she was happy, in a way very happy.

"That's true."

"May I see you again?"

"Yes. Call on Friday morning. Here's my extension at work, and my home number."

She took a crisp paper napkin from the next table, and with a ballpoint pen, wrote in both numbers. Her fingernails were red, and her leather gloves, with her perfume, caused a scent kin to nostalgia, which warmed him. Her eyes were gray, and very clear, nose strong at the arch, proud, and her dark brown hair getting gray was the way women getting older wore it more and more, short and choppy in a kind of French style, close to the head, becoming with her rouged cheeks, and round, plump lips. Her mouth was moist, forward above her jaw, predatory, yet her hands caught his eyes, for her skin was pale, white, and soft, she had hands that knew how to touch, he—looked closer. Dimples! Tender, plump fingers, with dimples on the knuckles, his eyes glowed: *she had hands like Titian's Venus.*

"Maybe get together Saturday afternoon?" As if feeling her touch.

"Yes, for a walk."

They rose on cue, waiter handing him the bill, which he glanced down at, and as he removed paper money from a clip, she left the tip, both having noticed, for the place so inexpensive, there wasn't much difference between.

He gazed out at traffic, as he paid at the register, in the clamor of the family, and mother, who gave him change with a soft sneer.

"Come again," she murmured.

"We will," he smirked.

Stepped to the front door, which he opened, and followed her outside, buttoning his topcoat.

"Continue," he said, "the story about that fascist artist, and the young woman."

They walked west, and she began . . .

"Yes, well, it's fascinating." Paused. "She's a pretty young woman with character, rather tallish, but well built, slender-waisted, and were it not for her feminine features, her body is that of a boy's, like the clothes she wears: boots, jeans, plaid shirts. No makeup, no jewelry of any kind except a Cracker Jack ring Joe gave her as a child."

"Why?"

"To hide her woman's body. We do that: wear oversize, awkward looking dresses, sweaters, sweatshirts, shirts, in the wrong colors, even appear frumpy."

"In fear of being seen by men?"

"In fear of being desired by men who are strangers, and to feel safe and at ease."

"I'm . . . a bit lost."

"No matter what is accepted as real, no matter how the world is, as she saw it, and sees it, but is beginning to want her freedom from it, if she couldn't merge with and be in the flow of those trumpets, and that big band beat in his blood, and him wounded, if she wasn't a guy, she'd be his secret body, even in herself, to astonish, and surprise him."

"Wow."

They stopped on a corner, with the light their way, waiting for a city bus to take a turn, before crossing. Though it was early in the afternoon, the sun was low in its winter sky, and blazed down on their faces.

Stepped up onto a curb.

"Imagine it!" she exclaimed.

Turned to him, her face flushed, excited —

"Night or day or whoever knows, on a warm noon in a high field, she gave herself to him: took off the boy's clothes, and gave him her woman's body."

"Yes, I see. Breathtaking."

"Which she had never given Joe."

"And?"

"This small, lazy blue fascist because he *is* lazy because laziness is fear of change, which terrifies him, so he has become in that sense a cripple, at home, going nowhere—"

"Reminding her of Joe."

"Yes! shedding the clothes of a boy, a girl becomes an adoring woman: passionate for him alone, her full, naked body, in his embrace."

"*At last.*"

Dimpled fingers took his hand.

Venus.

Walking west on the city sidewalk, shadows long behind them.

Printed January 1995 in Santa Barbara
& Ann Arbor for the Black Sparrow Press by
Mackintosh Typography & Edwards Brothers Inc.
Text set in Baskerville by Words Worth.
Design by Barbara Martin.
This edition is published in paper wrappers;
there are 200 hardcover trade copies;
100 hardcover copies have been numbered & signed
by the author; & 26 lettered copies are
handbound in boards by Earle Gray each signed &
with an original drawing by Fielding Dawson.

Photo: Susan Maldovan

FIELDING DAWSON was born in New York on August 2nd, 1930. Grew up in the midwest. Went to Black Mountain College 1949–1953. Drafted. Served two years in the Army. Since 1956 has lived in New York. Author of 20 published books. Chairman of PEN Prison Writing Committee. An exhibiting artist with the Jack Tilton Gallery in New York. Writes a column for the *Mendocino County Outlook*. On Thursdays reads letters from prisoners, on WBAI/Pacifica radio: The Morning Show, hosted by Bernard White. He teaches Creative Writing in Sing Sing.